Cynthia looked around for her belongings

Her heart was light and happy, even after the evening they'd spent fretting over Ryan's fever.

Tom followed her to the front door, a genial look on his face. "Thanks for helping me out tonight."

For a moment his eyes met hers and held, transmitting a need that went far past anything required by his son. A jolt of awareness went through her. For the first time she had a sense of what an incredible responsibility he had taken on alone. "I'm just glad he's okay."

"So am I."

Silence fell between them again. She was supposed to remain emotionally detached, impartial, but looking into Tom's eyes, she felt anything but. Worse, he started to lean toward her, his lips seeking hers.

ABOUT THE AUTHOR

Cathy Gillen Thacker is a full-time novelist who once taught piano to children. Born and raised in Ohio, she attended Miami University. After moving cross-country several times, she settled in Texas with her husband and three children.

Books by Cathy Gillen Thacker

HARLEQUIN AMERICAN ROMANCE

102–HEART'S JOURNEY
134–REACH FOR THE STARS
143–A FAMILY TO CHERISH
156–HEAVEN SHARED
166–THE DEVLIN DARE
187–ROGUE'S BARGAIN
233–GUARDIAN ANGEL
247–FAMILY AFFAIR
262–NATURAL TOUCH
277–PERFECT MATCH
307–ONE MAN'S FOLLY
318–LIFETIME GUARANTEE

HARLEQUIN TEMPTATION

47–EMBRACE ME, LOVE
82–A PRIVATE PASSION

HARLEQUIN INTRIGUE

94–FATAL AMUSEMENT
104–DREAM SPINNERS

Don't miss any of our special offers. Write to us at the following address for information on our newest releases.

Harlequin Reader Service
901 Fuhrmann Blvd., P.O. Box 1397, Buffalo, NY 14240
Canadian address: P.O. Box 603,
Fort Erie, Ont. L2A 5X3

MEANT TO BE

CATHY GILLEN THACKER

Harlequin Books

TORONTO • NEW YORK • LONDON
AMSTERDAM • PARIS • SYDNEY • HAMBURG
STOCKHOLM • ATHENS • TOKYO • MILAN

For Julie,
the sunny/stormy pathfinder in the family,
who has proved time and time again
she has only to set her heart and mind on something
to achieve it

Published March 1990

First printing January 1990

ISBN 0-373-16334-7

Preface

Several years ago I became fascinated by birth order and the influence it had on an individual's personality and career. The result is my Texas Trilogy—about the Harrigan clan. *Meant to Be* is Tom Harrigan's story. A bestselling novelist, he is the firstborn son, a high achiever who thrives on being in control. He likes structure and order, and chose a profession—mystery writing—that requires strong powers of concentration and staunch mental discipline.

As a child, Tom walked and talked earlier than his siblings. He thrived on his parents' attention and was quite close to them. He felt considerable pressure to perform, to set the standard for the other children in his family. Most of the time he succeeded. Because of this, he is confident in his abilities, but also very reluctant to do anything halfway. An inveterate procrastinator, he does something one hundred percent or not at all.

And that, for Tom, is where the trouble starts. He waits so long for the perfect woman that he remains a bachelor well into his late thirties. Fearful he has missed his chance to marry and have a family, he decides to have a child alone—via surrogacy. Tom knows from the beginning it is a risky endeavor, but he is confident he can pull it off. And for a short while, he does.

But then human nature, the fierce desire of a mother to nurture her own child, comes into play. And suddenly for Tom his world is turned upside down. Everything he holds near and dear is threatened.

Chapter One

"It's very important I understand what you're thinking," Tom Harrigan said significantly to the moderately attractive young woman seated across from him.

Sally Ann Anderson shrugged indifferently, letting him know the third degree didn't bother her in the least. "Ask whatever you feel you need to, and I'll answer," she said calmly, the serenity in her unblinking blue eyes underlying her words.

Again, impatience and a vague uneasiness shifted through Tom. Resisting the urge to loosen his thin silk tie and unbutton the first button on his azure blue shirt, he got up and paced the conference room with restrained, measured steps, which were very unlike his normal long, athletic strides. A regular office environment had always made him feel hemmed in; today that effect seemed doubled, making him long for the sanctuary of the wide-open spaces Texas provided in abundance, or even the cluttered old-fashioned study in his Dallas home where he spent most of his days writing bestselling mystery novels under the pseudonym Harrison James.

Sighing, Tom looked out the window at the traffic on the Central Expressway before turning back to Sally Ann. Although he had no qualms about the wisdom of seeking a surrogate mother to bear his child, he knew he had to be careful about the motives and expectations of everyone involved. Especially those of the surrogate.

He didn't want anything to go wrong in the process, and that meant being very sure of her motives. As for himself, he had no doubts. He wanted a child and although he had long since given up on his search for the perfect woman to settle down with, he hadn't given up the idea of being a father. Having someone to carry on the Harrigan name, someone to love. The sense of family was very important to him, and he knew it was past time he had a family of his own. Before too long, he'd be too old to participate in the raising of a child from infancy through the teenage years, and then onto college.

Typically once his decision was made, Tom pursued the idea relentlessly, going after his goal with the same tireless zeal he pursued everything else. He was confident he would achieve his goal, too; perseverance always paid off.

Tom studied the friendly, down-to-earth woman in front of him. He knew from reading her statistics she was twenty-seven, eleven years younger than him. "Why would you do this for me?" he asked quietly, intent upon her answer as he once again took the seat opposite her.

Sally Ann sent him a confident smile, not the least bit intimidated by him. A well-groomed intelligent-looking young woman with an impressive candor, she met his assessing glance head-on. "I'm a nurse. I've seen the surrogacy arrangement work in the past and work well. If people like me don't participate the whole program will be wiped out, and that would be a shame. Besides, you're a nice man. You deserve to have a child."

"You sound so sure of yourself." Still, he had to be very certain of her feelings. He didn't want anyone hurt in the process.

Sally Ann relaxed in her chair. "I am sure of myself."

Tom studied her. "You don't have any qualms about giving the baby up once it is born?" he asked quietly.

"No, I don't," she said serenely.

He sat back in his chair, aware that the psychiatrist evaluating Sally Ann, while not contributing much to their conversation, was carefully monitoring every word spoken during the mutual interview session. "How can you be so certain?" Tom asked, studying her youthful freckled face.

Sally Ann hesitated. She had come straight from her shift at the Dallas hospital as a nurse in the oncology ward, and she was still wearing her starched white uniform. "Because I've done this before," she said after a moment, once again meeting Tom's eyes. "It was a few years ago, when I was married. My husband and I were weathering some tough times financially." She sighed heavily, remembering. "You see, I had just graduated from college, and had my school loans to repay. Meanwhile, my husband, Billie, lost his job in the oil fields. His unemployment ran out before he could find more work, and he had to take a job he hated. And in the midst of all that I unexpectedly became pregnant. It was a difficult time for us, made worse when I lost the baby in my fourth month.''

"I'm sorry," Tom said, sympathizing with the hurt he saw on her face.

Sally Ann nodded, accepting his sympathy stoically. "Anyway, after that things went downhill," she continued pragmatically, knitting her hands together on her lap. She shifted restlessly in her chair. "My husband got laid off again. Our savings dwindled and we stood to lose both our house and our car. Surrogacy seemed the only solution. So I carried a child for someone else, and then used the money to get us out of debt.

"Unfortunately by then, the strains of the previous months had done irreparable damage to my marriage. We got divorced." This was said with sadness.

"I'm sorry," Tom commiserated gently.

Sally Ann lifted her chin. "Don't be. It was for the best. Billy's working for an oil company in Alaska now, and I have a good job with a hospital here in town."

Tom studied her quietly. Like himself, Sally Ann had dark hair and dark blue eyes, and was tall and athletically built. She also had a fresh-scrubbed, girl-next-door look about her, complemented by her friendly manner. As far as physical characteristics went, the two of them were a good match. But he couldn't shake the feeling that Sally Ann hadn't yet told him everything. "Then why would you want to be a surrogate again?"

Tom asked. "For the money?" He hated to be so blunt but he had to know.

She nodded and added dryly, "Like all nurses, I'm overworked and underpaid. The extra money would enable me to take a sabbatical. I'd like to travel."

"What about your job?"

"I've already talked to the hospital. They'll keep it open for me."

He still sensed she wasn't telling him everything. "Is that the only reason?"

She looked unhappily at the psychiatrist and then back at Tom, elaborating. "I have a physical condition—endometriosis, in which uterine tissue spreads to the organs outside the womb, the Fallopian tubes, the ovaries. It eventually causes infertility. I've taken medication for it, but it hasn't done much to control the condition and I don't want surgery."

"There's no cure?" For a moment, Tom felt her distress.

Sally Ann shook her head. "None. The most we can do is slow it down. Pregnancy will keep it from progressing."

"So by becoming pregnant—" Tom began.

"I'm buying myself some time," Sally Ann interjected. "Keeping myself in child-bearing condition a little longer than would otherwise be possible, while at the same time not assuming the responsibility of raising a child at this point in my life."

Tom felt relief. She would get something out of this arrangement, too, besides money—the possibility of having her own child in the future if and when she did remarry.

"I'm not completely without demands, though," Sally Ann continued. "For my peace of mind, Mr. Harrigan, I'd want regular reports on the child through a third party. I'd also like spot checks by the social workers here, so I can always be assured the child is safe and well. The child would also need to be provided for in the event of your death, and I'd prefer the guardian to be a married couple, not a single parent."

Tom appreciated her forthrightness. And on a gut level, he understood her emotional need to insure the safety of the child. "That's no problem," he assured her calmly. "I have a sister and a brother, both married, who're already excellent parents." Tom looked at her curiously. "Both would be happy to assume guardianship of my child, in the event of my death. I am surprised, though, that you wouldn't want to be named guardian." After all, it was her child, too.

"No," she said. "I don't want to be involved emotionally." She paused, her expression hardening as she laid out a second set of conditions. "I want to be under general anesthetic when the baby is born. And I want no contact with either you or the baby after the birth. In fact, I'll be immediately transferred to another floor after the birth, and dismissed from the hospital as soon as possible afterward. I don't ever want to see any pictures of the baby. Nothing."

Tom could understand her need to cut herself off emotionally from the birth, that under the circumstances it was probably the best thing she could do to protect herself. "Is that what you did in your previous surrogate birth?" he asked. He thought, if he were a woman, he would have had to make similar arrangements.

She nodded. "Yes. And I think that's one of the reasons I was able to act as a surrogate."

He could tell she meant every word she said. Relief flowed through him and relaxed his long limbs.

"And it doesn't bother you—the idea of giving up your child?" Tom pressed. These were hard questions, but questions that had to be asked. To his left, the surrogate-agency psychiatrist was busily scribbling notes.

"Maybe a little, but it's nothing I can't handle."

Tom appreciated her honesty. "Do your future plans include having children of your own?" Technically, Tom knew her answer had no bearing on his decision. Still, for his own peace of mind he needed to know.

For the first time during the interview, Sally Ann looked uncertain. "If I can find the right man to marry, yes, I will," she said softly.

"And what about in the meantime? Do you think you'll have more children as a surrogate."

Sally Ann shrugged. "Maybe, but only if I need to buy myself some more time and only if I can find someone I'm comfortable with."

"If you decided not to get pregnant again now— what would happen then, with your disease?" Tom asked.

Again, Sally Ann looked unhappy. "Then I face eventual infertility, perhaps even a hysterectomy to control the endometriosis. Neither remedy is what I want."

"Why not just have a child of your own then, and raise it on your own?" the psychiatrist asked, wanting to discuss other options in depth. "You'd accomplish the same thing—without having to sacrifice your child in the process."

Sally Ann sent the man a level look. "Because I don't want to be a single parent. It's too hard, too time-consuming, and besides I'm too involved in my work for that." She paused thoughtfully. "Any child of mine I'd want to raise as a full-time parent at home."

"Do you find your work in the oncology ward depressing?" Tom asked curiously, remembering she worked with cancer patients. Maybe it was because he was a novelist and was prone to abstract thinking, but he could understand the need Sally Ann might have of wanting to bring life into the world when constantly confronted with death.

"No, I don't," she said gently, and then went on to explain how she had come, through the course of her work and her religious beliefs, to accept death as part of the life cycle. Something to be met with dignity, as comfortably as possible, and without fear.

As she talked, Tom couldn't help but admire Sally Ann. She seemed so selfless. Nonetheless, he had to be careful.

Consequently, Tom and the surrogate met several times over the next few weeks and finally all were satisfied with the arrangement. The surrogate agency and the psychiatrist gave their stamp of approval. Niggling legal details were smoothed out. A contract was written up in which Sally Ann agreed to have artificial insemination and carry his child. In return, he promised to pay her fee and meet with all her conditions.

Everyone was happy. Especially Tom. Finally, it seemed, his lifelong dream of becoming a parent was about to come true. And eleven months later, Ryan Thomas Harrigan was born.

SALLY ANN CLIMBED into the wheelchair with the help of a nurse's aide. She was unaccustomed to the role as patient rather than nurse and was still shaky from the lingering effects of her unexpected illness. Had it been only ten months since she'd been here for the birth of Tom Harrigan's child?

Time had gone by so quickly. She'd worked for a while and then gone to Europe for a memorable six months. But no sooner had she landed in Dallas than she started running a fever. Two days later, the flu-like symptoms increased and she had gone to the doctor. She had an acute pelvic infection, and her physician had hospitalized her within the hour. Unfortunately, the infection had not responded to antibiotics, and the peritonitis spread. Four days later, she'd lost a great deal of weight and strength, and her fever had spiked to 104. She hadn't wanted surgery, but in the end the doctors had had no choice. To save her life, they'd performed a hysterectomy. She was infection free now, but the damage had been done. She was sterile.

She knew she ought to feel grateful she was alive, but all she could focus on was her inability to bear another child. Considering how much she'd done to stay fertile—even going so far as to have a surrogate child for someone else—made her fate all the more unfair.

They reached the ground floor and the lobby doors slid open. The aide wheeled Sally Ann out onto the floor, then went back to get the cart full of flowers from friends, and her belongings.

Sally Ann waited patiently, in no hurry to get home. And it was then that she saw Tom Harrigan coming in the entrance to the far right. The entrance led to the complex of doctor's offices in the medical center's west wing.

His tall handsome figure was unmistakable, and he looked harried and upset. The baby was cradled in his arms and wailing his heart out.

Hearing the sound brought tears to Sally Ann's eyes. Furious with herself, she brushed her tears away with the back of her hand and fought to get her emotions under control. But try as she might, she couldn't take her eyes off Tom Harrigan or the baby in his arms. Dressed in a navy-blue jacket and matching cap, the eleven-month-old, his eyes red from crying, appeared flushed with fever. He probably, Sally Ann thought, had some variation of the winter flu that had recently hit Dallas. The same flu she'd thought she'd had.

As Tom waited for the elevator, Sally Ann hurriedly wheeled herself in the opposite direction. She felt pursued, the hairs on the back of her neck oddly stiffened in fear. She couldn't, mustn't, let herself get near....

WITH RYAN SNUGGLED contentedly against his shoulder, a battered Snoopy clutched in one tiny fist and a little blue blanket in the other, Tom rocked slowly back and forth in the heavy wooden rocker. He could feel by the gradual relaxing of his son's sturdy twenty-pound frame that he was almost asleep. Humming softly, Tom continued to rock.

The medicine for Ryan's ear infection was finally working. Tom had never felt so helpless or worried as he had when Ryan had first started to cry inconsolably, without apparent provocation, earlier that morning. At first, Tom hadn't had a clue as to what was wrong; he only knew he'd never heard Ryan cry in quite that way before—as if he were bewildered, panic-stricken and angry all at once. By the time Tom had rushed Ryan to the doctor's office an hour later, Ryan had a fever.

Not surprisingly, Ryan hadn't cooperated with his pediatrician during the exam. It had been all Tom could do to keep the infant calm, while he paid for the doctor's services, and trekked to the drugstore to fill Ryan's prescription. The hours afterward had proved equally demanding and harrowing, showing once again that the job of a single parent was no easy task.

Still Tom wouldn't trade the experience for anything.

He could still remember the first day he'd walked over to the hospital nursery, and viewed his son through the glass. Tiny, red-faced, with a head full of fine dark hair, and dark blue eyes, Ryan had been the spitting image of Tom as an infant. Everyone had said so. But even if he hadn't looked like him, Tom knew he would've loved Ryan on sight. There was something special there, something deep and moving he couldn't explain.

Together they had managed just fine the past few months. Of course, he hadn't known much about diapering or feeding or soothing a baby with colic. But he had learned. Now those skills were as automatic to him as breathing. And just as deeply ingrained were the memories of Ryan's first smile, his cooing and laughing. Soon Ryan would be walking on his own. He already had his first two teeth. And he was learning to talk—or at least trying.

Ryan was growing up. Too fast.

Tom felt a lump form in his throat. He didn't want this moment to end. Holding on tighter to his son, he realized he felt very protective. Fiercely paternal.

Ryan sighed, his body becoming relaxed. He was asleep now. Tom could put him down. But for some reason he didn't want to. He wanted to hold him just a little while longer. He wanted to hang on to the moment.

If that was silly, so be it. It was just the way he felt because moments like this were too few and precious. Since Ryan had come into his life, his work and his career, although still important, had taken a back seat. He had been given a chance to experience a miracle, and he wouldn't take it lightly.

"FEELING BETTER NOW, aren't you, buddy?" Tom asked Ryan cheerfully as he heated Ryan's cereal several days later. Now that the fever was gone entirely, Tom could go back to work. He was anxious to put some of his ideas for his work-in-progress onto the computer. As soon as Ryan went down for his morning nap, Tom would head for his study.

"We're having oatmeal and peaches for breakfast this morning," Tom continued conversationally, taking the dish out of the microwave.

"Da!" Ryan said as he banged his hands enthusiastically against the plastic high-chair tray. He kicked his legs and waved both arms in anticipation of his morning meal, chattering and yelling, "Da!" all the while.

Tom grinned, feeling proud as a peacock. Of course, Ryan said "da" for everything at this stage of his life, but it was his first word, after all.

The doorbell sounded.

"Guess we better get that," Tom said. Ryan stilled and looked curiously in the direction of the door. "I know, sport," Tom said, "it's unusual for us to have visitors this early in the morning." He glanced at the clock. Eight-thirty.

Ryan held up both arms, indicating he wanted to be picked up. Tom smiled and obliged, then headed for the door. On the other side of the portal stood a distinguished-looking older gentleman, briefcase in hand. He handed Tom his business card.

"I'm Myron Singleton, an attorney here in Dallas." Tom blinked, and the older man continued smoothly, "I represent Ms. Sally Ann Anderson."

The name of the woman who had given birth to his son hit Tom like a fist in the solar plexus. He stared at the man. What could Sally Ann want? he wondered. He had been sending the reports of Ryan's progress to the third party—his lawyer—as initially requested. There'd been some home visits from the surrogate agency's social workers and psychiatrist, all tests he and Ryan had passed with flying colors.

Sally Ann couldn't have anything to complain about in terms of Tom's treatment of his son, or his love for Ryan. So what . . . ?

Mr. Singleton remained where he was, his expression cordial. Maybe too cordial, Tom thought. "May I come in?" Myron Singleton asked.

Tom's first impulse—albeit a decidedly juvenile one—was to say no and slam the door in his face. But he knew he had to hear this man out. A wedge of fear cutting through him like a knife, Tom stiffly nodded his assent. Okay, he'd let the man in. Listen to what he had to say. There was no reason to panic. No reason at all. Probably this was just some legal formality. Something that had been overlooked earlier. No one was going to try to take his son away from him.

Oblivious to Tom's panicky thoughts, Mr. Singleton sat down on the sofa and opened the briefcase on his lap, then removed a stack of papers. "I wanted to talk to you informally first, before we filed suit—"

"Whoa. Hold it right there," Tom said, raising a hand. His grip on Ryan tightened as he sat in the rocker across from Mr. Singleton. "What are you talking about?"

Mr. Singleton's expression sobered. "Sally Ann has had a change of heart," he said, a cold note of finality in his voice. Tom started to protest but Singleton cut him off. "Her circumstances have changed. She feels she made a mistake in signing away all parental rights to her son. She wants a reversal."

Tom stared at the man numbly, hardly able to believe what he was hearing, and yet knowing in his heart with a sick feeling of dread that his worst nightmare was starting to happen. Part of him could even understand it, maybe in some dark corner of his soul even anticipate it. After all, who wouldn't want Ryan? He was bright and lovable, with dark hair and blue eyes.

But Ryan was his son. His, and his alone. He was the one who had raised Ryan. He was the one who had sat up with him when he was sick, who had bathed him and fed him, rocked him to sleep every night. He was the central person in Ryan's life, the parent Ryan counted on and loved back as fiercely as Tom loved Ryan.

Singleton continued mercilessly. "She wants joint custody of her son, Ryan Thomas Harrigan."

"No..." Tom said hoarsely.

"I'm afraid so, Mr. Harrigan," the lawyer replied, his expression hard. "And she's prepared to sue you if that's what it takes."

For a second Tom was too stunned to act. His mouth suddenly had a metallic taste. His heart was pounding. He couldn't shake the hope that this was all just a bad dream from which he'd soon awaken.

Ryan squirmed in his arms and Tom's grip relaxed. Clearly sensing something amiss between the two adults, Ryan turned his back on Singleton and buried his face against Tom's neck. He wrapped his arms around Tom's neck and held on tight. "No," Ryan murmured, cuddling close and mimicking his father.

No! Tom thought. Ryan had actually said no! But his joy at discovering his son knew a second word was dimmed by the unfolding drama. How dare Sally Ann do this to him, Tom thought furiously, especially after all this time. How dared she do this to Ryan! And on a selfish whim!

His heart filled with the sickening sense of betrayal, he rose stiffly to his feet. "She can sue me, but it isn't going to help," he warned tightly. "I'm not giving up custody of my son."

Chapter Two

"Thanks for dropping by on such short notice, counselor," Judge Mitchum said, as Cynthia Whittiker took a seat opposite him in his chambers.

Cynthia smiled back at her well-respected colleague, feeling as at home in the formal, richly masculine setting as she did in her ice-green suit.

A successful lawyer, she'd had occasion to argue a good number of cases before the forty-eight-year-old judge. She'd found him to be a very pragmatic man, sometimes stern. He was also the devoted father of five, and a very busy man. He wouldn't have called her in person unless he had something confidential and sensitive. Her antennae were on full alert.

"I have an interesting and difficult case coming up in my court." Replacing his glasses, he looked straight at Cynthia. "It involves a surrogate-mother contract. The surrogate has changed her mind about giving up the baby to the father. She's suing him for immediate joint custody."

Cynthia sagged in her chair. The controversy and complications were enormous. It was the kind of case any lawyer would want, and Cynthia was no exception. "How old is the baby?" Generally speaking, the younger the better for all concerned, she thought, already digging in. Cynthia loved legal dilemmas, but she hated to see people in pain. Invariably, she ended up feeling it, too. And in a case like this, there were bound to be some hurt feelings. Things could get very unpleasant.

"He's eleven and a half months old," Judge Mitchum answered.

"Where do I fit in?"

"I need to appoint a legal guardian for the baby. With your extensive background in family law, you were the first person I thought of."

Cynthia sighed. She couldn't deny the case intrigued her on an intellectual level. To date, with the exception of the Baby M case, the laws surrounding surrogate motherhood had not been tested. To be a part of this case would be to partake in history. Emotionally, however she didn't relish the idea of being in the middle of a battle over a child. Still, she was well equipped from a legal standpoint to help the child.

"Have you met the people involved?"

"Yes, briefly. The father is a novelist here in Dallas. The mother's a registered nurse."

"What about the baby?" she asked.

"The baby is currently living with the father, although there's a hearing coming up to test that arrangement."

Cynthia could imagine how betrayed the father must feel. After all, he'd had a contract, guaranteeing that the child was to be his. Yet she could also imagine the anguish of the mother. This was her child, too, a part of her flesh and blood.

"I see. What's their marital status?"

"Both are single." Judge Mitchum reached into a file on his desk, and produced a photograph. "This is Ryan Thomas Harrigan, the child in question."

Cynthia scrutinized the photo. Ryan had a headful of thick, dark curly hair, inquisitive blue eyes. His rounded cheeks had a healthy pink glow. His body was sturdy, the picture of health. He was a very cute baby, and judging from the happy expression on his face, very well tended.

Privately, Cynthia felt surrogate contracts should be outlawed. The whole idea was too close to baby-selling for her taste. But that wasn't the question being debated. The point was that the child was there, and needed to be protected from the quarreling between his biological parents. "When do I start?" she asked.

Judge Mitchum smiled, relief easing the lines in his pleasantly craggy face. "I was hoping you'd say that, counselor. You can start right away."

As Tom maneuvered his Bronco through the late-afternoon traffic on the Central Expressway, he thought about the meeting ahead of him. He knew very little about Cynthia Whittiker, except that she was supposed to be fair. He wondered what she would look like, if she would be older—grandmotherly—or someone young, fresh out of school. He supposed it didn't really matter as long as she was on his side.

Meanwhile, now that the custody suit was becoming a reality, his ability to concentrate on anything but his son was next to nil. The damned custody suit had disrupted his life, threatened everything he held near and dear. And it was all going to get worse, much worse, before his prayers were answered.

Of course he would win, Tom reassured himself firmly, as he guided his Bronco down the next exit ramp and eased into the slower traffic. He had that signed contract on his side, for one thing. He'd lived up to his part of the bargain. It was only fair Sally Ann live up to hers.

Nevertheless, it infuriated him to realize that because of Sally Ann's reckless change of heart, Ryan now had a court-appointed legal guardian.

His gut churning with the emotions this initial interview was generating, Tom parked his car in the lot outside Cynthia's office, and got out. Ryan had drifted off to sleep during the car ride and Tom woke him gently, then talked soothingly to him while he lifted him from the car seat, grabbing the diaper bag with his free hand.

It was five-thirty, and Cynthia Whittiker's office was deserted except for a slim woman in her middle thirties. Was this Cynthia Whittiker? She couldn't have been further from the grandmotherly lawyer he'd been hoping for. He paused, his chest tightening as he took in her sophisticated clothing, the gold streaks in her shoulder-length chestnut hair. Closer in age to him than he had expected, she was an attractive woman, with a sunny countenance and steady hazel eyes.

Remembering once again why he was there, he felt himself stiffen defensively. Her hazel eyes tracked the movement, but her expression remained inscrutable.

"Hello," she said, extending a hand, taking charge of the situation. Her handshake was firm and welcoming. "You must be Tom Harrigan. I'm Cynthia Whittiker." She dropped her hand and turned her attention to Ryan. "And this must be Ryan."

Tom nodded, his mood edgy now that they were getting down to business. All too aware of Cynthia's scrutiny, Ryan began to squirm in Tom's arms. Shyly, he turned away from her and buried his face in Tom's neck. He linked both arms around Tom's neck and held on tight.

For a moment, Cynthia focused on the way Ryan was clinging to him. Tom thought he saw a flash of disapproval on her face, which was quickly replaced with lawyerlike neutrality.

"Please, come in. Have a seat," Cynthia said cordially as she led Tom and Ryan past the reception area into the private office beyond. A large comfortable-looking rocking chair sat in one corner. Tom was surprised. "I have a lot of parents with babies," she explained. "I've found a rocking chair makes the appointments go a little easier."

Maybe she was more qualified than he'd first judged, Tom thought, impressed. "Do you have children?" he asked, before he could think. She certainly acted as if she were comfortable around kids. Was she married? Now that he looked, he didn't see a gold ring on her left hand.

"No, but I have a lot of relatives who do and I enjoy spending time with all the kids in my extended family." As she sat down, the edges of her long jacket opened to reveal more of the white satin blouse beneath. She crossed her legs and her knee-length skirt slid halfway up her thigh. She was nice to look at, he thought, with her full breasts and long, perfectly shaped legs. Her hair looked silky and her skin glowed with health.

Tom turned to the matter at hand. "So, what happens now?" he asked. His lawyer had explained to him that Cynthia would be interviewing him and Sally Ann, to determine their fitness as parents. He just wanted to get it over with.

"I guess we begin. So, do you want to tell me about yourself, and about Ryan?" Cynthia said, turning on the tape recorder on her desk. Her hazel eyes narrowed slightly as she turned back to him. Her voice was still warm, husky, inviting confidences. "About your life together?"

No, Tom thought, sighing inwardly, he didn't want to tell her anything, but since there was no avoiding it, he took a deep breath and began.

Long minutes later he concluded, "... and since he was born, I've managed quite well on my own."

Cynthia weighed what Tom had told her with what she observed about Ryan. It was true, the baby did seem happy, and on the one hand, it seemed a shame to disrupt that. But he had also been deprived of any contact with a mother. Something all children needed, she felt, remembering how close she had always been to hers.

Aware he was watching her relentlessly, she dropped her gaze and shuffled some papers on her desk. Her job would have been a lot easier if he weren't so attractive. With his rugged good looks, he probably could've had almost any woman. And yet he'd chosen to go this whole parenthood route alone. Why?

"You know the judge has asked me to make a recommendation about the baby's placement from now until after the custody trial takes place, Ryan could stay with you, with his mother, or in a foster home."

At the last two alternatives, Tom stiffened visibly. The strained look around his eyes increased. In that second, she saw how vulnerable he was. His emotions, at least where his son was concerned, ran very close to the surface. Too close for Ryan's good? Was he going to be able to handle this? she wondered. And how would she react if he couldn't?

"My lawyer told me about the temporary custody hearing," Tom said finally. "Has a date been set yet?"

Cynthia felt pressured, just thinking about it. "January 30." That was only two weeks away. And yet Ryan's immediate fate—the decision of where he would live temporarily—rested in her hands.

"And the actual custody trial will be held . . . ?"

"April 12."

"There's no way to speed this up?"

Cynthia shook her head. "I'm afraid not."

"Terrific," Tom muttered.

Cynthia glared at him. His sarcasm she didn't need.

Picking up on his father's displeasure, Ryan dropped the bottle of juice he'd been holding and began to twist around, until he could see Tom's face.

"I'm going to do the most thorough job possible," she said in an effort to reassure him. Even though it means I'll probably feel like I'm in the middle of a firestorm the whole time, she added to herself.

After a moment, he nodded stiffly, then his angry eyes met her. "My attorney explained the nature of your job to me."

For some reason, he put her on the defensive. She had to get back to the subject at hand—him. "You don't seem very happy about this," she observed.

"And I suppose you would be in my place?"

Touché.

"I'm sorry," he said. "That was uncalled for."

The compassionate core of her longed to say something to comfort him. But on a professional level she knew she couldn't do anything of the sort. There was simply no telling how this situation would turn out. Especially since Ryan might quickly get just as attached to his biological mother as he already was to his father. And it was that eventuality she had to make possible and work through, before she could even begin to figure out what might be best for the child.

"I know this situation is tough for you, Tom, and I'll try to make it as easy on you and Ryan as I can, but I still have a job to do here. And that means I have to observe Sally Ann with Ryan, too. See how they interact." Not giving him a chance to protest, Cynthia continued determinedly, "I've asked her to come by the office today. In fact, she should be here any minute."

Her announcement was met with utter silence as Tom's brows rose and lowered like twin thunderclouds. The temperature in her office was cool, yet Cynthia began to perspire.

"May I stay?" Tom said finally, his voice husky.

"I'd rather you didn't," she said briskly, but patiently. She avoided his eyes, concentrating instead on the carefully combed layers of his dark brown hair.

"It'll be easier for me to observe them, if it's just the two of them," she said. "For today, anyway, I only need thirty minutes."

Tom's jaw set protectively. He shifted in his chair, his broad shoulders straining against his blazer. "But Ryan doesn't even know her!" he protested, his eyes holding hers in a silent plea.

"Exactly his mother's point, I believe."

"I want to be here," he said firmly. "This time, at least."

"No." Silence fell between them, but she refused to back down. This wasn't her decision, but the court's, and she refused to take any gruffness from him.

"Look, I know he hasn't met Sally Ann. But that can be easily remedied." Her voice dropped persuasively as she continued, "Children are very adaptable, much more so than adults. It'll be all right, Tom," she reassured, "I promise." Just then the outer door opened, and they both rose as Sally Ann walked in. Seeing Tom, Sally Ann looked briefly frightened. She stepped back a pace, swallowed hard. "H-hello, Tom."

Tom merely nodded.

Cynthia's feelings of impending doom increased.

Sally Ann took a deep breath and looked back at Ryan. Then, her expression as stubborn and determined as Tom's, she turned to Cynthia. "I hope I'm not too early," she said by way of greeting.

Cynthia glanced at her watch. Sally Ann was ten minutes ahead of schedule. "That's all right. Come on in." As Sally Ann tiptoed in, Cynthia opened a drawer and removed a net bag of brightly colored plastic baby toys. She walked over to Tom and held out her arms. Ryan glanced at Cynthia, then the toys. He looked interested, but still didn't budge.

Furthermore, Tom didn't look like he wanted to surrender the child. Cynthia bit back a sigh. Maybe she should have been prepared for Tom's uncooperative attitude. For Ryan's sake, Tom should be making this easier for them all, not harder; after all, he knew darn well there was no getting around the situation.

Finally, Sally Ann backed away slightly and sat down in an armchair against the far wall. She looked lost, hurt, very much in need of a friend. Cynthia's heart went out to her, too. It couldn't be easy for Sally Ann. She must want her son back very badly to be willing to go through this ordeal. But then, wasn't that how mothers were?

Deciding there'd been enough stalling, Cynthia reached for the baby, who protested audibly the moment she touched him. Nonetheless, she persevered. Talking soothingly to Ryan all the while, Cynthia inclined her head toward the door, silently indicating Tom to leave.

Again, their glances meshed. She felt for him, but she had a job to do. Evidently he realized that. Tom stood up reluctantly and drawled "I'll be right outside," then left the room.

Still holding Ryan in one arm, Cynthia opened the net bag of toys with the other. Ryan looked in the direction his father had gone, then back at the bag. For a moment, Cynthia thought he was still going to let out a prodigious wail. But then curiosity got the better of him. He thrust a hand into the bag, then pulled out a bright red plastic ring, which he examined avidly, turning it this way and that.

Pleased at the way the session had started out, Cynthia suggested softly to Ryan's mother, "Why don't you sit in the rocking chair?" Smiling encouragingly, she continued gently, "Then, once you're settled, I'll hand him over."

FORTY-FIVE MINUTES LATER—Sally Ann had left moments ago—Ryan relaxed in his father's arms, some of the toys still clutched in his tiny fists. He leaned his head against his father's chest. Tom held his son close, a look of contentment mixed with relief on his face.

"I thought the first visit went well," Cynthia said with as much calmness as she could muster. She was relieved it was over, too. When Tom, Sally Ann and Ryan were together the tension was unbearable.

Tom looked up, his brows pulling together. "My son belongs with me."

"This is only the first of many visits," she warned. "Ryan will have plenty of chances to bond with Sally Ann before the final custody is decided. You can't interfere with the court's intentions."

Tom's lips clamped together. "I don't care how many visits they have. But as you know I'm countersuing for sole custody."

That, Cynthia already knew. She was curious to know how he rationalized his actions to himself. He didn't appear to be selfish, just extremely protective of his son. "You'd deprive your son of a mother, when he could have one?'' She thought Sally Ann's request for joint custody was not so unreasonable.

Tom sighed and ran a hand through his hair. "I want him to have a stable life, not be shuttled back and forth from one home to another, like a child from a broken home. From everything I've seen, that's rough on a child. I don't want that kind of life for Ryan. I want him to be happy and secure and I just don't see how that's possible with joint custody."

Cynthia shared his concern. Granted, joint custody could work well—but when the parents didn't get along or agree on how a child should be raised it inevitably created a conflict-filled environment. She didn't want to see Ryan or any child subjected to that kind of emotional turmoil, if it could be avoided.

"So you have no sympathy for Sally Ann at all?" Cynthia asked, aware her tape recorder was still going, and all this would later be transcribed and made available for Judge Mitchum.

"She had no interest in Ryan at all—none—for the first eleven months of his life," Tom countered, avoiding Cynthia's question. "Why now?"

"Because as you know, she became sterile."

Tom softened some. "I understand that. Still a contract was signed and she could have followed his progress without seeking parental rights."

Cynthia sighed, convinced the conflicts were too complex to solve in a single afternoon.

Tom accurately read into her divided loyalty. "My son belongs with me," he repeated firmly, gathering up Ryan's things and handing Cynthia back the toys she'd provided. "And I'll battle to the end."

Chapter Three

"I know we're supposed to conduct these sessions in your office," Tom Harrigan began the following week as Cynthia greeted him at her office door, "but it's such a pretty January day—why not go to the park? They have a nice sandlot for the kids as well as some baby swings."

He glanced at the lawyer's outfit, his gaze lingering momentarily on the jade broach pinned to her breast pocket, before returning to her face. "I thought maybe we could take Ryan there," he plunged on, "and talk while he plays. I know you have a lot of questions to ask me today."

"Yes, I do—three whole pages of questions, as a matter of fact," Cynthia said.

She hoped he would be more open with her than he had been at the previous meeting. Although she supposed it was natural for him to have his guard up, it was imperative he be totally honest with her about his feelings and his life-style if she were to get to know him in any real sense.

He sent her a quizzical glance and she explained the nature of the questions. "We're going to cover your current living situation." Cynthia glanced down at her dressy black skirt and frowned. "I don't have anything here at the office to change into, though."

"No problem." He sent her a sexy grin. "I've got a couple lawn chairs stashed in the back of my Bronco. I, uh, figured you wouldn't want to mess up your clothes."

"Or yours," Cynthia said, thinking he really did look nice today. Some men wore a shirt and tie as if the businesslike attire was choking them. Tom looked perfectly at ease, and handsome enough to grace the pages of a magazine.

"So you'll go?"

Try as she might, she couldn't find any harm in the idea, this once. Ryan would probably be happier and more content, and as long as she gathered all the pertinent information to make an informed decision before the temporary custody hearing, Judge Mitchum would be satisfied.

"Sure, why not." Swiftly, she gathered up her notebook and tape recorder, then went to the closet, and removed a pair of black flats from a box on the shelf, which she slipped on in place of her high heels.

Tom grinned. "Better?"

She nodded. "Much."

He fell into step beside her as they left her office, promptly adjusting his strides to the shorter length of hers. She appreciated his gallantry.

"We can take my Bronco," Tom said, holding the door open for her as they left the building. "Afterward I'll drop you back here."

Feeling maybe they were getting to be too familiar with one another, she said, "That's not necessary."

"I know." Tom shifted Ryan into his left arm, and then reached into the pocket of his trousers and rummaged for his keys. "But it'll be easier."

Cynthia couldn't dispute that. It would also give her a chance to see what kind of driver Tom was. Maybe she was being silly, not wanting to be confined in close quarters with him. After all, it would only be for a few minutes. "Okay," she said finally.

As Tom settled Ryan into the back seat, Ryan, obviously no stranger to going places in the Bronco, gurgled happily, waving his arms and legs.

As it turned out, she very much approved of the way he handled the jeep. He drove sedately, sticking precisely to the speed limit, taking no unnecessary chances as they blended easily into the late-afternoon traffic. Surreptitiously, she made a note of this in her book and then another to remind her to observe how Sally Ann drove, too, at some point. She wanted her observations of the two to be as balanced and fair as possible. Tom must have some shortcomings, she thought, and it was up to her to find them, not to be dazzled by his good looks, or his chivalry, or the love he had for his little boy.

At the park, Tom settled Ryan in a deserted corner of the sandlot with a plastic shovel, sifter and pail. Cynthia helped set up the two webbed lawn chairs. "So when is Sally Ann's next visit?" he asked, taking a seat beside her. He stretched his legs out in front of him. Cynthia was uncomfortably aware of their proximity to one another. Trying to appear nonchalant, she shifted her chair, both to allow herself more leg room and have a better view of Ryan.

In the distance, Cynthia noted a long-haired man in a Hawaiian shirt and loose khaki trousers taking pictures of the people enjoying the unseasonably warm day. He looked like a professional.

Aware Tom was waiting for an answer to his question, she said, "I meet with Sally Ann tomorrow afternoon." Turning her attention back to Ryan, she watched as he dropped his shovel and wiggled both hands in the sand, gurgling happily. She couldn't help but grin at him.

"Not today, after me?" Tom asked, his eyes leaving Ryan to focus on hers. He looked edgy again, upset, and he sat forward slightly on his chair. The long-haired photographer began making his way toward them.

Cynthia shook her head. Tom's scrutiny was making her uncomfortable, but not wanting him to know, she held his gaze without blinking and answered calmly, "No. I realized it puts her at a disadvantage, having to follow you. The baby gets too tired. I think it would be better, for us all, if we did the interviews on alternate days."

Before she could say anything else, the photographer was in front of them. "How ya doin'. Jeff Thorpe here." He reached over to shake hands with Tom, and then nodded at Cynthia. "I'm with the *Dallas Daily Sentinel*." He peered at Tom. "Say, aren't you that novelist? Uh, Harrison James? The one who writes mysteries? That Bond-type stuff?''

Tom nodded and smiled graciously. Jeff grinned. "I knew it! Say, want some free publicity? One of my photos is going on the front page tomorrow. Might as well be of the three of you." He looked at Ryan, who was still digging happily in the sand. "This your kid and, uh, wife?" He looked back at Tom. "You know, I could've sworn you weren't married."

"I'm not. Cynthia's a friend. And thanks for the offer, but I don't want to be in the paper."

"How about your son?"

"No," Tom said quickly. "No pictures of Ryan. Or me," he added.

"You sure?" Jeff pushed. "I might be able to get my boss to add a line or two about your new book, your being a local celeb and all. The publicity couldn't hurt. We've got half a million subscribers, you know."

"Thanks, but I don't think so." Tom smiled graciously again.

Jeff shrugged. "Okay. If that's the way you want it. Ma'am. Nice seeing you." Turning, Jeff Thorpe sauntered off.

Cynthia became aware her heart was pounding. "You handled that well," she said. *Better than I did.*

Tom frowned. "I just hope he doesn't start nosing around, trying to find out who you are, in the mistaken idea that there's romance between us."

Cynthia flushed. "Why would he think that?"

"We're here together, aren't we? Apparently playing hookey while we both tend to my son? You're an attractive woman…and not very long ago his paper put me on their most eligible-bachelor list, so…''

Cynthia bit her lip. For Ryan's sake, as well as for Tom's and Sally Ann's, she wanted to keep this custody battle quiet. But it wasn't just Ryan and Tom she was protecting. She was protecting herself, too. She didn't want her name linked with Tom's romantically, because that could hurt them all in the upcoming custody battle by undermining her credibility as a professional.

Tom leaned forward and put a hand on his son's wrist, stopping a shovelful of sand that was halfway to Ryan's mouth. "No, Ryan," he said gently. "We don't eat the sand. It's yukky."

At the word yukky, Ryan made a face. Tom handed him the sifter, and showed him how to use it. Ryan accepted the new toy and promptly began to sift the sand. Cynthia liked the gentle but firm way he interacted with his son. She had always felt you could tell a lot about a man by the way he treated a child. Without warning, she wondered what he would be like as a lover. Would he be as gentle as he was with his son? Or more complex than that, more passionate? He seemed to be holding a lot inside. She sensed he would be likely to release that flood of feeling when he made love to a woman.

Irritated with the way Tom predisposed her to fantasizing, she gave herself a mental shake. "So, where were we?" she asked brusquely, looking down at her notes.

He frowned. "We were talking about the interviews. You wanted to set them up on alternate days."

"Right."

"It's going to be harder for me, if we set it up that way. I don't have that much time to work as it is. I devote so much of my day to Ryan that it'll cut even more deeply into my writing time."

"Which is usually when?" Cynthia asked, taking notes.

He shrugged. "Depends on where I am in a particular book. In the early stages of a book, I write maybe four to six hours a day, then spend another two hours or so researching and thinking about plot and characters. Once I get an entire manuscript roughed out, I work longer hours. Usually an hour or two in the morning, when Ryan first gets up and is content to stay in the playpen in my office. Later when he naps, I usually get a good two to three hours in, and then I always put in about four or five hours straight in the evening after he goes to bed at seven."

"You don't hire a sitter?"

"I've found I don't have to. Of course it doesn't leave a lot of room in my life for much else these days."

She sensed a sadness beneath his anger. "And you haven't wanted to go out, either, have you?" she guessed softly.

"Ryan's my life." He choked up briefly and turned his glance to Ryan, then at the gradually sinking sun. "My whole life," he repeated in a husky tone.

Realizing he needed a few moments to compose himself, Cynthia remained quiet and watched Ryan play. Looking back at Tom, she saw how the late-afternoon sun brought out the red and gold highlights in his hair and lent a golden hue to his skin. She was all too aware of what an attractive man he was. Under different circumstances, she would have probably tried to get to know him not as Ryan's father, but as a man.

She forced her thoughts back to the situation at hand, and the particular problem of arranging the next visit with Ryan and his mother. "Would you prefer I come to your house and pick up Ryan?"

"No, I'll bring him to your office," Tom said, his expression relaying his disapproval of her decision. And then the pain he felt, and the resentment—not of her, but Sally Ann.

Cynthia checked to make sure her tape recorder was still running, for now they were getting to the heart of things. Tom's ability to control his emotions would play a major part in the custody battle. "You don't like Sally Ann much, do you?" she asked levelly.

"She's only involved in this because she was paid to be," he pronounced harshly. "I'm the one who wanted a child."

"Nonetheless, Sally Ann played a big part."

Tom pivoted to face her. "Physically, yes, but not emotionally, and I guess that's what's bothering me the most. The fact that she could be so pragmatic, so clinical about it all then, and yet now be anxious to be Ryan's mother."

"She did give birth to him, Tom."

He struggled to stay controlled, levelheaded. "I appreciate what she did for me very much, because without her there would be no Ryan. But as for everything else, I just keep going back in my mind to the months during her pregnancy, her attitude. She was so removed, Cynthia."

Something of Cynthia's confusion and disbelief must've shown on her face, for he said, "Oh, she showed up for the artificial insemination and went through the ordeal of being pregnant—something for which she was well paid, I might add—but as for becoming emotionally involved with the child during her gestation, she didn't. She thought of herself as an incubator. Do you realize she didn't want to see him after his birth? The entire first eleven months of his life, she never showed the slightest interest in Ryan. That's why I mistrust her attitude now, because I'm not sure how she is going to feel about Ryan, about wanting to mother him eleven months from now! And I can't bear the idea of him being hurt, of being rejected."

That, Cynthia could understand, but she also knew Tom's memory was selective. "That was your agreement, was it not? That Sally Ann not become involved or ever think of Ryan as anything but *your* child?"

"Yes. And now she wants to renege. Well, it's too late."

But Sally Ann didn't think it was too late, Cynthia thought. And in the years to come, Ryan might not, either. In fact, there'd probably come a time when he'd want very much to have a mother. Calmly, Cynthia said, "She probably wouldn't have, if her circumstances hadn't changed, if she hadn't become sterile."

"That doesn't help me much, does it?" Tom turned to face Cynthia more fully. Ryan was toddling over, and he reached down and picked him up, settling him on his lap. "Ryan, is *my* son," Tom said softly, as he lovingly ruffled Ryan's hair. "He belongs with me, and only me."

"You have no sympathy for Sally Ann?"

Tom stopped in the act of dusting the sand off Ryan's pants. His face hardened. "She knew what she was getting into when she signed that surrogate contract."

"But she didn't know she would be sterile," Cynthia repeated softly.

For the first time that day Tom looked regretful. "I'm sorry about that. I really am. But that doesn't mean I want her near Ryan," he finished stubbornly.

"You may not have a choice," she said cautiously, knowing there was an excellent chance Sally Ann would win the legal battle to be a part of her son's life. She wondered how Tom would react if the judge awarded partial custody to Sally Ann, or even permanent visitation rights. Would he be able to handle it?

The tinkling music of an ice-cream truck filled the air. All three turned in unison as the truck pulled into the adjacent parking lot. Ryan giggled and pointed. "Da!" he said. "Da da!"

"You want some ice cream, don't you, sport?" Ryan nodded a vigorous yes. Tom glanced at his watch, noting it was nearing dinnertime, then caved in.

"I guess it's okay. Cynthia? Would you like something?" Tom was already setting Ryan back down beside his pail and shovel. While Ryan went happily back to his digging, Tom stood and reached for his wallet.

Cynthia's stomach rumbled, reminding her how long it had been since lunch. Ice cream was something she never had been able to pass up. "Sure," she said, grinning, a little relieved something had happened to diffuse Tom's stormy reactions to her questions about

Sally Ann. She reached for her handbag. "I want chocolate topping, and here's some money..."

"It's no bother."

Cynthia held out a crisp dollar bill and pressed it into his palm. "I insist." Under the circumstances, she couldn't accept anything from him, lest it be considered bribery. Surely he knew that!

His eyes darkened. "Fine," he said simply, his face expressionless.

Tom returned moments later with a soft drink for himself, a cup of vanilla ice-cream for Ryan, and a vanilla cone with chocolate topping for Cynthia. They moved to a nearby picnic table. Ryan sat on Tom's lap, happily eating the ice cream his father spooned into him. Watching, Cynthia's mood mellowed again. She couldn't help but admire the free-flowing love and tenderness between father and son.

It would be a shame to break that up. But Sally Ann had rights, too, she reminded herself. In fairness, those needed to be explored.

"If the court were to decide on joint custody," she asked, "how would you feel?"

He looked at Cynthia grimly. "I'd fight it all the way to the Supreme Court if necessary." His voice was quiet but deadly. "We had a contract. And I damn well expect Sally Ann to honor it."

She sighed, wishing this were easier, that Tom hadn't chosen such an unyielding stand. Because in doing so he had only made it harder for all of them.

"SO HOW'S IT GOING?" Tom Sr. asked later the same day, after Tom had put Ryan to bed.

Normally Tom saw his parents only every month or two. But lately, with all the trouble in his life, his parents, as well as his younger brother and sister, had taken to stopping by whenever they were remotely within range of his Dallas home. Tonight his parents had come by, after visiting some former teammates of his father's on the Houston Astros, who were now residing in nearby Fort Worth. They'd brought a new stuffed animal for Ryan, and a box of bakery goodies for their son. Tom appreciated their concern and support more than he could ever say.

"All right, I guess." He faced his father, amazed that the newly retired sportscaster could look so fit, his close-cropped silver hair the only sign of age. And even that lent him a distinguished air.

Rachel Harrigan, Tom's mother, walked into the room carrying a dessert tray. After sending her son an affectionate glance, she began doling out cups of coffee and chocolate-chip cookies. "This court-appointed guardian," Tom Sr. continued, taking a seat next to his wife on the sofa. "Cynthia what's her name?"

"Whittiker."

Tom Sr. studied his son. "Is she being fair?"

Tom sighed. The last thing he wanted to do was worry his parents. At their age, he felt they ought to have nothing but happiness; they'd certainly earned it. Hence, he chose his words carefully. "I don't think there is such a thing as fairness in this situation, Dad."

"Then let me rephrase that." Tom Sr. sat forward, resting both elbows on his knees. "Is she on your side?"

"It's hard to tell. She's, well, she's an attorney. You know how inscrutable attorneys can be."

Tom Sr. frowned, clearly disappointed. Tom knew his father felt there was nothing his eldest son couldn't do if only he put his mind to it. That expectation had rankled when he was growing up, and continued for years afterward, mainly because Tom felt that no matter what he did, on some level it was never good enough, that his dad, especially, was always expecting him to do better.

"You haven't been charming her?" Tom Sr. persisted.

He didn't want to disappoint him, but he didn't want to be pressured either. "I've tried. But every time she brings up the subject of Sally Ann...I start to lose it. I'm just so angry, Dad. So incredibly angry." He knotted his hands into fists. Without warning he felt near tears, and that, too, was unlike him. He never cried, never bashed his fists into walls, or slammed things around. Now he wanted to.

"You have every right to be angry," his father concurred bluntly. He slanted a look at Rachel, and seeing she was worried, too, put his hand over hers. "Although your mother and I feared all along this would happen," Tom Sr. finished wearily, squeezing his wife's hand.

Rachel Harrigan had been quiet up to now. Given an opening, she spoke her mind. "I never felt any woman could really give up her child, not when it came right down to it."

Tom remembered bitterly how they had counseled him against hiring a surrogate to bear his child from the very beginning—which, to him, was ironic in the extreme. As the firstborn son, growing up, it had been drilled into him relentlessly to go after what he wanted with no holds barred. And he had—always—in everything he'd ever attempted.

His parents had always approved. Until he'd wanted a child without a wife.

"Son, I think it's time you got yourself a team of high-powered lawyers. I've gotten some names from my friends at the Houston Bar Association." Tom Sr. pulled a list from his pocket and handed it to his son.

Although he knew his father meant well, Tom didn't want his help. Nonetheless, out of politeness, he perused the list. He recognized them all as theatrical geniuses who, in his opinion, belonged more on the Broadway stage than in the courtroom.

Tom handed the list back. "Dad, if I hire any of these lawyers, the trial'll turn into a media circus."

"Maybe not. Especially since the judge ordered the records sealed to protect Ryan."

Tom felt his whole body tense. "Yeah, and you know how long that vow of secrecy lasted in the Baby M trial a couple of years ago."

"That was different," his mother cut in. "It wasn't the lawyers who broke that story."

"Sally Ann might be the one to break this seal of secrecy," Tom Sr. said. "After all, she's reneged on just about everything else. Who's to say she wouldn't go to the press with her story?"

Tom was quiet. He'd been duped before by the freckle-faced nurse, with her down-home air, and the twang in her voice. His mood darkened as he thought about what a media circus might do to his son. "She'd better not," he said.

Tom Sr. forced the list of high-powered attorneys back into Tom's hand. "I really think you need to get yourself a hotshot."

Tom shook his head and his father's face darkened angrily. For the first time in his life, Tom felt the full sting of his father's disapproval, which had generally been reserved only for his younger brother, Mike— when Mike was acting his worst. "Okay, ignore my advice. But prepare yourself to lose Ryan. Because unless you do something smart like this now, Sally Ann will win custody—mothers always do."

"This isn't the usual case," Tom argued.

"No, it's not, but I'm not sure that'll make a whole lot of difference in the end. Face it, son. Sally Ann Anderson is an upstanding citizen just like yourself. And unless you can prove otherwise, figure out some reason she shouldn't have partial custody of Ryan..." Tom Sr. let his voice trail off unhappily.

"This is the nineties, Dad. Fathers have rights, too. Parenting isn't something that is sexually determined. Both men and woman are recognized as capable of raising children."

"We aren't disputing that, Tom," Rachel cut in, trying to make peace between the two men. "But to some people, motherhood is sacred." She paused, her blue eyes filling with tears. "We didn't want you to get into this in the first place, mainly because we feared something like this might happen. But now that you have, we don't want to see you hurt. We love Ryan..." Her voice caught and she couldn't go on.

And to lose my son, Tom thought darkly, *would destroy me.*

Suddenly, he didn't want to hear anything more about his lack of judgment. "Thanks for stopping by to see me," he said quietly to his parents, giving them a none-too-subtle hint it was past time for them to leave. "I appreciate it. I know it was a long drive for you."

Tom Sr. hesitated, looking as unhappy as Tom felt. Rachel, the family peacemaker, intervened. "It is late, honey. We should go."

"All right. You'll call us if you need anything?" Tom Sr. asked, as his son walked them out.

Tom nodded. But even as his parents drove away, he knew he wouldn't call them. Oh, he knew his parents loved him deeply, but they didn't support him anymore, not really. No, they saw him as a fool, and that perception hurt.

Tom knew just how much he had given up in settling for the idea of having a child via a surrogate. He'd shelved his lifelong dream of having a wife he loved, and children with her. Not because he didn't still want that, but because he despaired of it ever happening. Clichéd or not, all the good women his age seemed to be already married, or at least involved. Most of the marriageable women were too young. Realizing his chances of finding his ideal woman were poor, he had settled instead on having his own child.

Unfortunately, his parents seemed to think, although they were far too tactful to ever come right out and say it, that Tom was only getting what he deserved for ever embarking on such a risky endeavor.

And that being the case, he was afraid the new rift between them was permanent. Because right now he couldn't afford to have anyone in his life who didn't support him one hundred percent. And that included his parents.

KNOWING SHE HAD TO CHECK OUT the home environment of both litigants before the temporary hearing on January 30, Cynthia drove to Sally Ann's apartment after work. The brick and frame building was fairly new, but there were several problems Cynthia spotted right off. For one thing, the complex's swimming pool was not equipped with a lifeguard. There were plenty of sidewalks and parking spaces, but no places for children to play. Cynthia also noted that it was on a rather busy street near the hospital.

Sally Ann answered the doorbell on the first ring.

"Hi," Cynthia said cheerfully, glad she'd caught Sally Ann at home. "I'm here to check out your living situation."

"Come on in." Sally Ann moved to let her pass. "I guess this is the surprise visit you warned me about," she said. Although it was early evening, Sally Ann looked fresh and rested, Cynthia noticed; she'd still have plenty of energy to give to a child.

"Your apartment is cozy. I like the way you've decorated it," Cynthia said, seeing the handmade afghan on the sofa and cheerful needlepoint pillows. The furniture was modest but dust free, the carpet swept, the kitchen clean and orderly. Ditto for the master bedroom.

"Let me show you Ryan's room," Sally Ann said.

She led the way to the spare bedroom. It had recently been painted a pale yellow. There was a new crib and changing table; curtains, crib sheets and baby blankets in a cheerful teddy-bear motif. A rocker sat in one corner of the room.

"I still have to get a stroller and a car seat and some books and toys for him," Sally Ann said. "And if I do get custody of him, I'll probably move to a more child-oriented complex or a house with a yard. My lease is up on May first."

That took care of the negatives outside, Cynthia thought. "You're really serious about having him with you, aren't you?" she asked, impressed.

"I made a mistake giving him up," Sally Ann said firmly. "But I'm going to make it up to him. My only remorse is that Tom has to be hurt." She bit her lip. "I know that, all this unpleasantness aside, he really is a nice man. He feels threatened now, and I guess that's understandable, but I think he'll come around. I think—" her eyes met Cynthia's earnestly "—that he and I will be able to work out a joint-custody agreement."

Privately Cynthia wasn't so sure. Still, Tom didn't want to see his son hurt, and time had a way of healing most anything. She only prayed she would have the wisdom to assess the situation fairly and make the right decision in the end.

They walked back into the living room. Seeing several framed photos on the parson's table in the corner, Cynthia paused to look at them. "My family," Sally Ann said, pointing out half a dozen brothers and sisters, and their spouses, her parents and several aunts and uncles.

They looked warm and friendly, and definitely of modest means and rural background. "How do they feel about what you're doing?" Cynthia asked.

Sally Ann hesitated. "I'm not sure they understand. They didn't really want me to be a surrogate, but it was something I felt I had to do..." Her voice trailed off.

"Do you see them often?"

Sally Ann shook her head. "No, they live in west Texas. I get back once or twice a year, but that's about it. We write, of course."

"You haven't ever thought about returning?"

"No." Sally Ann's voice was firm. "I like Dallas." She stared at the collection of photos. "I'd put a picture of Ryan here, but I don't have one," she said, "yet."

Cynthia heard the hope and determination in her voice and smiled. In all likelihood, Ryan could live with his mother very happily. Score one for Sally Ann.

Chapter Four

"I don't get why you're so upset," Toby Williams, of Williams and Sons Publishers, said the following day. He'd come to see Tom on business and had instead ended up talking about the unexpected local publicity one of his star writers had just gotten. "So your and Ryan's picture was on the front page of the *Sentinel*." He sat on the edge of his patio chair and watched as Tom continued making preparations for Ryan's first birthday party. "So what? Lots of parents—even celebrity parents—take their kids to the park."

Tom was silent, unable for the moment anyway to answer truthfully. Maybe if the custody trial hadn't been secretly underway, Tom wouldn't have felt so invaded. But with everything that was at stake... Cynthia Whittiker had been in that picture, too. Furthermore, she'd been identified, last name and all, which meant Jeff Thorpe had gone out of his way to find out who she was. Fortunately, as of yet, anyway, the tenacious photographer had no idea why the three of them had been together. Tom didn't want the local media making his son's custody trial the feature story on the evening news.

"I asked Jeff Thorpe not to take the photo," Tom explained patiently as he hung up a streamer that said Happy Birthday Ryan Harrigan!

"Yeah, and he took the photo anyway because you're famous, a local boy who's done good. Big deal." Toby took a second look at the picture. "They mentioned your last book, didn't they? Great! What I'm curious about is the gorgeous lady sitting next to you. An attorney here in Dallas. New girlfriend?"

A dedicated bachelor at thirty-five, Toby was also a tireless lady-killer. He liked to joke that no woman was safe in his path, and with his aristocratic features, white blond hair and gray eyes, his expensive clothes and prep school manners, there were few who were.

Normally Tom couldn't have cared less whom Toby pursued. But seeing him ogle Cynthia sent a surge he couldn't name through him.

"You didn't answer my question, Tom," Toby prodded, bringing him back to the present. "Is she your girlfriend?"

He could see why Toby was so captivated. Cynthia looked even prettier than he remembered her being that day, with her soft chestnut hair blown slightly around her face, a delicate smile on her lips....

"She's just an acquaintance," he said vaguely.

Thus far he hadn't told Toby about the custody battle. For one thing, there was no reason for his editor to know. Second, the judge had sworn them all to secrecy for Ryan's sake. Only the people involved, and their immediate families, were to know.

"Not your type at all, right?" Toby said, deadpan.

Tom could tell Toby knew that wasn't true. Cynthia was exactly his type. In fact, had she not been Ryan's guardian, he probably would already be in pursuit. But under the circumstances that hardly mattered. No, what counted here was what was going to happen to Ryan. And the first thing he had to do was throw Toby off the track.

Tom decided to change the subject entirely. "So, what was this idea you had about a series in Europe?" Toby had flown in from New York for the express purpose of talking to him about it.

Toby watched as Tom filled another balloon with helium. "I was thinking maybe five books. One each in England, France, Italy, Germany. Maybe Switzerland or one of the Scandinavian countries. You could take a trip to Europe, scope things out, get some ideas. The company will pay for it if you agree to do some promotion while you're there."

Three years ago, he would've jumped at the chance to do a series set in Europe. But now he couldn't even leave the country, and all because of the custody suit. Concentrating on the excuses he could use, Tom said, "Ryan doesn't have a passport."

Toby shrugged, unconcerned. "So leave him here. Your folks will take him for a couple of weeks, won't they?"

"If I asked, sure."

"But you won't."

"Look, the idea sounds great. I'd like to do it." Tom finished one balloon and picked up another.

"Great!" Toby countered enthusiastically, getting up to lend a hand, "but I need plot outlines right away."

Tom stifled a groan at the thought of all that work and another deadline. "Like how soon?" He tied a string of balloons to a fence post.

"Like next month."

"For five books?" Tom's mouth dropped open as he thought about the enormous amount of time and effort that would entail.

Toby shrugged. "I know it's a lot of work but the idea is hot. The budget's there to promote it. It'd mean a lot to my career, too, if we get the series under contract and make it a success."

Tom had to admit he liked the idea. Plot possibilities were already coming at him, but the task would still take a lot of time and effort. On the other hand, he had gotten his start at Williams and Sons Publishing. He owed the company—and his longtime editor and friend—a lot. "I'll need at least six weeks to come up with some outlines," he cautioned. "And even then they'll be sketchy."

"That's okay, as long as we have something. Uh, where do you want this stereo system hooked up?" Tom pointed to a small wooden table and Toby set to work connecting speakers and turntable. "What about Europe?"

Tom sighed. "Europe's going to have to wait," he said, as he spread a linen tablecloth over a folding table and began stacking presents for Ryan.

"You can get Ryan a passport in a day, you know, if you go to the passport office in person. You could hire a nanny. Take Ryan with you."

"Maybe later in the spring," Tom said. They could go after the final custody hearing April 12, which would be a nice break after the turmoil that was bound to come in the next few months.

"Fantastic!" Toby said, just as the caterers arrived.

Tom showed them where to set up and then, with Toby's help, went back to his own preparations for the party. Pending court case or no, he was going to give Ryan the best and biggest birthday bash a one-year-old could have.

CYNTHIA HEARD THE SOUNDS of revelry as soon as she got out of her car. Striding gracefully past the eight cars parked in front of his house and in the driveway, she headed for the tall wooden gate leading to the backyard. Tied to it was a strand of colorful balloons and the gaily printed message Happy Birthday Ryan Harrigan!

Smiling at the sheer ebullience of the handmade sign, she knocked, and when no one answered, opened the gate and slipped inside. What she saw then was no less than amazing. The extreme level of extravagance disturbed her. This wasn't a good precedent for Tom to set for Ryan, she thought, especially under the circumstances, when he knew, financially anyway, Ryan's mother couldn't begin to compete.

Taking a moment to get her bearings, she looked around, cataloging the display for future reference. A stereo had been carted out to the patio, and was playing "It's Not Easy Being Green," and other songs from *Sesame Street*. There were two clowns, a fellow twisting animal figures out of colorful balloons, and a three-tiered birthday cake decorated with Winnie the Pooh and Disney cartoon figures. Two uniformed caterers scurried about, and a huge stack of presents sat on the linen-covered folding table.

Tom Harrigan was happily supervising the festivities. Seeing Cynthia, he turned and started for her. She was struck again by his inherent sexiness. "Glad you could make it," he said gregariously, but his welcoming smile faded when he got close enough to see the disapproval in her eyes.

Feeling she'd given her feelings away, she quickly made her expression impassive. She didn't want to fight with him about this. It wasn't her place to advise him how to behave, simply observe what was happening, and then report back to the court.

Nonetheless, she knew his overindulgence would look bad to the court. And that, she did regret, for there was no denying he loved his son dearly.

Forcing a smile, she said, "Hi. I'm sorry to interrupt."

"That's okay," he said quietly. His eyes searched hers worriedly as he instinctively picked up on her mood. "What's up?"

Everything. "Actually, there are a couple of reasons I stopped by. First, I saw that picture of the three of us in the paper."

"You're worried about it, too."

"One of the society columnist's for a rival paper has already been making inquiries about what's going on between us—if there's a romance." She flushed a little as she admitted the last. It was easy to see why people would've jumped to that conclusion. They had looked a little too chummy in that photo.

"No one told them the real reason, did they?"

"At this point, no one aside from us really knows. Anyway, I've done my best to counter the rumors but I wanted to let you know they exist. If anyone were to call you, just say we're friends and leave it at that."

The worried lines around his mouth increased. "Do you think people will buy that?" he asked huskily.

Cynthia shrugged. "Probably—when time passes and they don't see us together again on a social basis, out at parties or anything. At any rate, I wanted to let you know we're doing our best to keep a lid on the whole situation."

"Thanks."

She lifted her hands, a dazzling smile on her lips. "It's my job. The second reason I'm here has to do with Ryan. You remember I once told you I'd be making a surprise visit to check your home environment? Well, this is it."

Tom frowned, sensing something amiss in her reaction to the festivities. He took a step nearer, his lean-muscled body exuding both power and inherent sensuality. The faint but tantalizing scent of his after-shave seemed to accentuate his masculinity and it was all she could do not to step away from him as he said quietly, for her ears along, "Couldn't you have picked a more normal time?"

Cynthia leveled her gaze up, away from the short-sleeved yellow polo shirt and well-fitting khaki trousers.

"It shouldn't matter what day or time I pick," she countered equably.

Without warning, the back gate opened yet again and Tom's hospitable grin faded. Sally Ann Anderson was standing there, a small gaily wrapped box in her hands.

"What's she doing here?" Tom hissed, giving Cynthia an angry glance. "Is this part of your surprise visit, too?"

"No," Cynthia said, angry at both Tom and Sally Ann. She started for Sally Ann, with Tom right on her heels. "In fact, she's not ever supposed to come here at all," Cynthia whispered to Tom, hoping to calm him down.

Until the court could decide custody, Sally Ann's visits with her son were to be strictly chaperoned and prearranged, always held with Cynthia's approval and in her presence.

Sally Ann knew that, yet she had broken the agreement. Why? Surely she knew this wouldn't bode well for her. Darn it, why did these adults have to let their emotions drive them? Why couldn't they act with some forethought?

"Hello." Sally Ann offered Tom a tentative smile, which was not returned, before handing the package to Cynthia. "I just came by to drop this off," she explained nervously, never taking her eyes from Tom's dark, forbidding glance.

"Sally Ann, you know you're not supposed to be here," Cynthia said firmly, stepping between the two.

"I know." Sally Ann's lower lip trembled and her eyes filled with tears. She looked strangely vulnerable, her face pale beneath the freckles. "But I just couldn't let it pass without doing anything at all. I had to bring him something to let him know I cared."

"If you really cared for Ryan, you'd have gone through Cynthia," Tom muttered, his jaw still rigid with anger. Sally Ann shot him a hurt glance.

Before Cynthia could intervene further, a lovely older woman joined the group. Introducing herself as Rachel Harrigan, Tom's mother, she said to Cynthia, "And you're . . . ?"

"Cynthia Whittiker, Ryan's court-appointed guardian," Tom replied.

"Oh." The color left Rachel's face.

"Ms. Anderson here was just leaving—" Stepping around Cynthia, Tom started to take Sally Ann's arm. His mother intervened. "Wait, Tom." Rachel looked at Sally Ann. "If you wouldn't mind, I'd like a word with you."

Rachel sounded civil: nonetheless, Cynthia had grave doubts about the wisdom of a conference between the two women. "I don't think that's wise under the circumstances."

"I think it will be all right," Sally Ann said. And then to Rachel, "Besides, I'd like to talk to you, too."

Tom looked at Cynthia with a mixture of annoyance and pleading. A muscle worked angrily in his jaw. "You can't seriously think to allow this!"

Unfortunately, nothing had been written thus far to forbid such contact. While Cynthia agreed with Tom, she had no legal reason to interfere. "I can't do anything to stop them from talking, but I warn both of you—no trouble. Especially not here. And not in front of Ryan.''

''There won't be any trouble,'' Rachel said smoothly, leading Sally Ann toward the patio doors. ''We'll go inside,'' she said, ''and talk in the living room.''

Tom glared after them helplessly. Cynthia was of two minds. The skeptic in her feared a clash of two opposing forces, while the hopeful part of her yearned for the two women to be able to reach an understanding of one another's viewpoint, and maybe even a quick solution to the problem of Ryan's custody.

''I'm going to go ahead with my spot check,'' Cynthia said, pulling out her notebook.

Tom strode off toward Ryan, leaving Cynthia to look around and mix with the party-goers.

After a few minutes a sudden noise caught Cynthia's attention. She turned in time to see Sally Ann slam out of the house and head for the gate. Silence fell as she departed. In the background, Ryan let out a howl. After a moment Rachel came out sad-eyed. ''I tried to reason with her. But . . .''

Tom swore beneath his breath. Without another word, he marched toward the party-goers. Cynthia and Rachel followed.

Tom was holding Ryan in his arms. And although it took him a minute to calm his son, Cynthia could tell that Ryan felt more secure with Tom there with him. She made a note of that, too.

The rest of the birthday bash for Ryan went without a hitch. Knowing she'd seen more than enough to fill out a preliminary report on Tom's family, Cynthia looked around for her purse. Tom stopped next to her on his way inside. "I'd like you to stay," he said quietly. "We need to talk."

Cynthia felt a sense of foreboding, but she agreed, hoping she was doing the right thing. After Tom had shown everyone out and paid the caterers, he said fiercely to Cynthia, "I don't want her ever dropping by here on the spur of the moment again."

"I agree, she shouldn't have done that, and I'll make sure she understands she's not to do it again," Cynthia said quietly. Sally Ann's impulsiveness in this instance was odd. Out of character.

"Well, see that you do," Tom said shortly. "Babies need structure in their lives, continuity to feel secure. I can deal with her visiting him on a regularly scheduled basis, but I can't and won't have her showing up every time I turn around."

Cynthia simply nodded and said, "Well, if that's all, I'd better leave you to your work."

"No, it's not all," he said. She stood motionless. "I want to know what you're thinking," he continued, stepping closer. "When you first got here and looked around, I saw the disapproval on your face." For a moment, hurt turned down the corners of his mouth. "You didn't like what you saw here today, did you?"

Cynthia hadn't expected this plea. Part of her wanted to give in, but another part knew she couldn't—not without compromising her position as Ryan's guardian. She lifted her chin and said rather stiffly, "It's really not my place to judge, Tom, but to simply report on what I see." *And then eventually make a recommendation that Judge Mitchum might or might not follow.*

He waved away her skillful evasion impatiently and said, his expression fierce once more, "I want to know what I did wrong, so I can correct it. What did you see here today that you didn't like? You were really turned off when you walked in. You hated everything about Ryan's party." His low voice now throbbed with hurt. "I think I deserve to know why."

Cynthia was silent.

"There's a hell of a lot at stake here, Cynthia. I'm not just asking for the sake of my ego, but for the sake of my son. If there's something wrong, if I've done something you think will hurt him, then you need to tell me what it is so I can fix it."

Cynthia sighed, unsure what to do or say. She wasn't used to having anyone see into her heart and mind so easily, never mind a man she needed very much to remain impervious to. "I would hate to see Ryan be spoiled rotten by you and your family," she said at last. "Sally Ann is never going to be able to compete with your lavish life-style on her salary. It would be very hard for Ryan and perhaps unfair to cope with two such diverse sets of circumstances."

"What? So I'm supposed to lower my standard of living to hers? Stop writing books?"

"No, of course not. On the other hand, you don't have to go so far overboard—the way you did at this party."

Tom flushed guiltily. "What else?" he demanded.

His defensive attitude made it easier for her to continue. "You can't buy a child's love, Tom. I've seen a lot of divorces, and dealt with children who've been traumatized by battling parents—parents who loved them. I'd hate to see you and Ṣally Ann get involved in a rivalry over Ryan." Yet she could see it was already beginning to happen, each parent in essence saying, "Love me more, Ryan, love me more."

He was silent, taking that in. When he looked at her, she saw the hurt and confusion in his eyes. "Is that what you think I'm doing?" he asked hoarsely.

"Not consciously, no," she said gently. Needing and wanting him to take a good look at what he was doing, she continued, "But maybe you do feel you have a lot to make up for. The lawsuit...putting Ryan in this position in the first place." She was trying to see if he'd gone overboard out of guilt, or if this was the way he would have acted regardless.

"First of all, I don't feel guilty about the custody battle. As for the party, I know it was spectacular. Birthday parties in our family always have been. It's the one time we pull out all the stops. But you're right, I hadn't thought about Sally Ann not being able to match that."

Cynthia looked at him with respect, liking the adult way he'd handled her criticism. And, as she studied the chiseled lines of his face, she realized that perhaps this class difference was something that might never be resolved. No one could pretend the differences didn't exist. They weren't Tom's fault or Sally Ann's; it was just the way things were. "As long as your heart was in the right place..." she said finally, studying him.

"It was," he reassured her bluntly, his expression contrite.

She nodded, wishing everything else were so black and white, so easily discerned. The temporary custody hearing was in two days. She would be expected to make a recommendation, based on her findings so far. Generally the courts liked to leave the child where he had been living for the duration of the trial, unless there was some reason—abuse or neglect—that necessitated the child's being moved promptly. Obviously that wasn't the case here, Ryan was well cared for by his father. But he had seen precious little of his mother to date. She was all set up to care for him, and it seemed unfair to deny her the chance, however short-lived, to become a real mother to Ryan. After all, Tom had already had Ryan for a year. Was it too much to ask for Sally Ann to have him for a few months, too? But the adults really weren't her main concern. Ryan was. She had to think about what was best for him. Was it fair to uproot him now, when he might be sent back to live with Tom again? Moving from house to house might be very confusing and upsetting for Ryan. Still, babies were very adaptable, much more so than adults. If she didn't ask that Ryan be allowed to live with his mother, how would Sally Ann ever bond with Ryan in the way that comes from living with someone? How would Ryan ever get to really know his mother? And didn't babies need the sustained love of both parents to really thrive? Would it be possible to ask for joint custody in the interim, Cynthia wondered, allow Ryan to live with both parents now? Was that idea workable, considering the hostility between Sally Ann and Tom?

She didn't know. In all probability, Judge Mitchum would go along with whatever she advised; thus Ryan's fate, and Tom's and Sally Ann's, rested in her hands. Cynthia frowned. This was a far more difficult decision than she had anticipated. And there was no way around the fact that her decision was bound to hurt someone.

CYNTHIA'S MIND remained on the custody dilemma as she said goodbye to Tom and drove across town to the rehabilitation center where her mother was currently recuperating from an auto accident. Deciding nothing could be gained now by further worry, she decided to concentrate on her mother, at least for the moment.

Delicate neurosurgery had repaired some of the nerve damage sustained during the accident but the mobility in her fingers was still limited. She had enrolled in rehab to help restore it fully. She was a flutist, and range of motion was critical. And Faith was hoping daily to someday be right back where she had been before the accident, and resume her work as a college flute professor.

"I didn't think you were coming tonight," Faith said as Cynthia walked into her room, a copy of the latest James Galway tape in her hand. In jeans, sneakers, and an oversize college sweatshirt, Faith looked as young as her college students. At fifty-three, her short curly hair was still a thick chestnut color, her green eyes radiant behind the funky blue-and-red reading glasses.

"Couldn't help myself." Cynthia grinned, determinedly warding off her mother's you're-doing-too-much-for-me speech. "Besides, I couldn't wait to give you this." She sat down in the chair beside the window and pushed the plastic-wrapped cassette toward Faith.

Her mother accepted the present with an exclamation of delight. "Cynthia, this is wonderful. Really. You know how much I love Galway."

"Want to listen to it now?" Cynthia asked, smiling.

"Sure, if you don't mind." Faith was already hopping out of her chair and striding energetically to the jam box she kept beside her bed. With a great deal of difficulty, she finally managed to unwrap the cellophane, take the cassette out of the box and slide it into the machine. Watching her mother fumble with such a small task was painful to Cynthia. It showed her how much farther her mother still had to go before she'd be able to play the flute again.

If anyone was born to play the flute, my mother was, Cynthia thought. *We just have to give her time.*

As the lyrical sounds of Galway poured into the room, Faith smiled. Picking up a small rubber ball, she sat cross-legged on her bed and began doing a series of hand exercises.

"Have you heard much from the people at the university?"

Faith smiled. Beads of sweat appeared on her forehead as she concentrated, trying without much success to wrap her fingers snugly around the ball. "Everyone's been very kind. Not a day goes by that someone doesn't show up from the music department." She grunted in frustration, relaxed her hand, and with a steely look of determination, tried again. "And, uh, a lot of my students have been by, too." She sighed. "I miss teaching them, that's for sure. But I've got an ex-

cellent person covering for me, so they'll do all right."
Nonetheless, for a second, her mother looked depressed.

Knowing how much pain she had been in, and how she had to fight every day just to be able to perform the simplest of tasks, Cynthia couldn't blame her. She, too, was depressed about her mother's condition. The accident had been a rotten break. But Faith was recovering. And she would continue to improve, Cynthia felt sure. She smiled at her mother. "You'll be back before you know it," she promised.

Faith nodded, but looked nowhere near certain as she looked down at the rigid fingers on her hand. "I hope so," she said softly. "I really hope so."

"WHAT IS YOUR RECOMMENDATION regarding Ryan Harrigan?" Judge Mitchum asked Cynthia.

It had been two days since the party, and now the group was gathered in his chambers. Sally Ann and her lawyer, Myron Singleton, were on one side of Judge Mitchum's desk, Tom and his lawyer on the other. Cynthia had a chair in the middle of the two parties, and she'd never felt more ill at ease. She knew how much she would be hurting at least one of them no matter what she said. But she had to do what was best for Ryan.

Keeping her gaze fastened on Judge Mitchum, Cynthia said, "I recommend that Ryan remain where he is." Beside her, Tom gave a sigh of relief. On the other side of her, Sally Ann gasped and tears welled up in her eyes.

She knew Sally Ann felt betrayed, and her heart went out to her. As calmly as possible, Cynthia continued, "Ryan is happy and healthy, well cared for. I think it would be a mistake to move him at this point."

"I've read your written reports," Judge Mitchum said, "and I agree that it would be in Ryan's interest to continue living in the environment he knows. Until the case can come to court for a full hearing on April 12, Ryan will remain with his father."

"I think, however, he needs more time with his mother," Cynthia continued pragmatically. "Much more time. She needs to see him several times a week—"

"With your supervision, of course," Judge Mitchum said.

"Of course." She didn't make this commitment lightly; she knew she was taking on a lot, but it was the only fair way to proceed.

Judge Mitchum nodded. "All right. Three times a week it is, then, for the next two and half months."

Tom conferred briefly with his lawyer. When they were finished, his attorney said, "If I may, I have a suggestion about the visitations." Judge Mitchum gave the go-ahead, and he continued, "We'd like Ryan's visitations to be conducted in Mr. Harrigan's home, rather than Ms. Whittiker's office."

"Wait a minute!" Sally Ann burst out. "That'll put him at an advantage if we meet in his house. I mean, I want to make things easier for Ryan and all, but at the same time I don't see how I can bond with him if Tom is always looking over my shoulder!"

"I won't be in the room with you, Sally Ann. I won't even be in the same part of the house. But I will be close by if he becomes upset or if any of you need me for something."

"Is that the only reason you're asking for this?" Cynthia said. Remembering how unwelcome Tom had made Sally Ann feel at his home during the birthday party, Cynthia shared Sally Ann's incredulity.

"No. All this running back and forth has gotten me behind in my writing. If we do it this way, then I can go back to my office during the visitations and get some work done. It'll also save me a lot of driving time, and be a little easier on Ryan."

Tom added reluctantly to Sally Ann, "I also think Ryan will warm up faster to you if he's on his own turf."

"Maybe you're right," Sally Ann said. "This probably would be easier for Ryan, and whether you believe it or not, Tom, I do want what's best for him."

A strained silence fell in the chambers. "It's all right with me," Judge Mitchum said finally. "Cynthia, how do you feel about this? Do you have a problem supervising visitations if they occur at Tom's house?"

"Well, no..." If the adults could rein in their animosity toward one another, she thought.

"Then it's settled," Judge Mitchum said, glancing at his watch. The meeting over, both clients left with their attorneys, Sally Ann still looking a little crushed that Tom had been awarded temporary custody, Tom looking not nearly as relieved as Cynthia had expected him to. After all, he'd just won round one.

"I'M SORRY IT TOOK ME so long to get back to you, but I've been in court all day," Cynthia said, late the following day. Because her secretary said Tom had sounded so frantic, and his house was on the route home, she had stopped by to see him in person.

"Did you see the article in the paper?" he said, leading the way into the family room.

"No. Why?" she asked, alarmed.

"Read for yourself." He handed her a folded section.

Quickly she scanned the page, finding a small article headlined: "Local Courts Try Case Involving Surrogate Mother..." Heartsick, stunned, she read on.

"They know about me and Sally Ann," Tom pointed out. "They just don't know our names. They're calling Ryan 'Baby R.' I don't know about you, Cynthia, but this makes me very nervous."

She bit her lower lip. "I wonder how they found out." The article was in the *Dallas Daily Sentinel*. Obviously the photographer hadn't made the connection. Yet.

"I was hoping you could tell me how they found out," Tom countered tensely.

Cynthia sighed and shook her head. "I'll call Judge Mitchum," she said. "We'll try to find out where the leak is and plug it."

"And if you can't?"

She swallowed. So much was at stake here. "We will."

She suddenly noticed how quiet the house was. "Where's Ryan?"

Tom's face softened. "He's napping. He had a long day."

The doorbell rang. "What now?" Tom picked up the newspaper and placed it face down on the captain's desk in the corner. "If you'll excuse me..." he said.

He returned seconds later, his father at his side. Tom Sr. had a newspaper in his hand.

Tom looked at her grimly. "Dad said that article was picked up by the wire service. It was in the Houston paper this morning, and God knows where else."

"I'm worried," Tom Sr. said frankly.

So was she. Unfortunately, despite the fact both men looked as if they were counting on her saving the day, Cynthia was not able to do more than make unfounded assurances that this wouldn't happen again. When she had finished, Tom Sr. looked at her but didn't say a word. Neither did Tom.

Sensing her presence was no longer needed, Cynthia said, "Well, I better be going. Call me if anything else happens, Tom. Otherwise, I'll see you on Thursday, when I bring the social worker from Family Services over."

He sent her a pained look and asked gruffly, "How long will the social worker be here?"

"Two hours. From five-thirty to seven-thirty."

"That's the dinner hour," Tom protested, "the toughest time of the day for any parent."

"That's why she wants to be here then. I guess she figures if you can handle Ryan when he's tired and cranky and hungry, then you can handle anything."

"It sounds like a test," Tom Sr. interjected, his expression unhappy.

It was, Cynthia thought. And privately she hoped Tom did well on it.

AFTER THE WAY SHE'D LEFT him on Tuesday, Cynthia expected Tom to be uptight when she took the social worker, Irene Johnson, to his home on Thursday evening. Instead, he seemed relaxed, greeting them at the door in jeans and a much-washed rugby shirt.

Cynthia made the introductions. To her relief, Tom and the fiftyish social worker hit it off right away. "Ryan's in the kitchen." Tom led the way to a sunny room at the rear of the house. "Hey, Ryan!" he said to the tyke strapped happily in his high chair. "Look who's here!"

Ryan banged a pretzel-shaped teething ring against his tray. "Hi," he said, and grinned.

Cynthia did a double take. "Was that what I think he said?" she asked.

"Yep. He's learned a new word." Tom gestured for them to take a seat at the table, then got them each a cool drink and went back to scooping blueberry-filled batter into muffin tins. Cynthia didn't know about Irene, but she was struck by his competence in the kitchen.

"We're going to have to eat while you're here, so you both might as well eat, too, unless you have other plans for dinner," Tom said cheerfully as he slid the muffins into the oven. "I'm assuming, of course, that you like tuna casserole."

"I love tuna casserole, but I'm surprised you like it," the social worker commented. "Most men don't."

Tom gave a lopsided grin that made Cynthia's heartbeat accelerate. "I admit I was never wild about it in my youth," he said with a roguish twinkle in his eyes. "My mother used to serve it for lunch a lot, and at the time all I could say was yuck as I washed it down with lots of milk. But all that changed when I was out on my own." He shook his head, remembering. "Tuna casserole was one of the easier things to prepare, and it was also one of the cheaper sources of protein. Important in my starving-writer days."

So he'd known his share of lean years, too, Cynthia thought, surprised. "How long did it take you to get published?" the social worker asked curiously.

"Five years," he said. "Five long years of writing during the days and tending bar at nights."

"And in all that time you never gave up?" Cynthia said, impressed.

Tom shrugged, and his eyes held hers as he answered, "I knew writing was what I wanted to do. I figured I would get a novel published eventually, once I'd learned the craft. Besides, it wasn't any great sacrifice for me. I love creating stories and characters and puzzles for readers to solve. Half the time it's more like recreation than actual work."

"And the other half?" she questioned.

Tom checked on the muffins. "The rest of the time it's just hard work. Incredibly hard."

Cynthia and Irene sympathized. There were days when they, too, would give anything not to have to do anything remotely connected to their professions.

"Did you write as a kid?" the social worker asked. Beside her, Ryan was busy playing with kid-sized measuring spoons and plastic bowls. Cynthia couldn't help but note how blue Ryan's eyes were, how much he looked like his father.

"Sometimes. For fun. And for school, too." Tom bent to pick up a toy Ryan had dropped. He washed it off, then handed it back to Ryan. "But back then I never figured I'd end up doing this as a career."

"When did you know?"

Leaning against the counter, he gave Irene's question some thought. "I guess it was my senior year in college—UT—when all my other friends were being recruited for jobs with big companies. I was a communications major and played on the college baseball team. There was some talk of my playing pro baseball, but I knew deep down that I wasn't good enough, nor driven enough."

Cynthia understood. Because her parents had both been musical geniuses, she'd always been expected to be a phenomenal musician, too. But she'd never had quite the talent or drive of her parents, and as a result, she'd been at best competent.

"What did your parents want for you?" Irene asked.

"My dad encouraged me to follow in his footsteps and go into sports announcing."

"But you didn't."

"No." Tom's gaze turned serious, and again he glanced briefly at Cynthia, too, and gave her a pensive smile. "I knew I needed to do what was right for me, and not just be a carbon copy of my dad. That's when it came to me that I might like to be a writer. You see, to escape all the pressure, I had been reading a lot of fiction, especially mysteries. After a while it got so thirty pages into the book I could pick out the villain. Thinking I could do better, I set out to write my own. From the first day at the typewriter—'' his grin widened appealingly ''—I was hooked.''

And so were a lot of readers, she thought. "How did your parents react to the news you wanted to be a writer?" Cynthia asked.

"They were surprised, but supportive. They just felt I should have been published a lot sooner."

The oven's buzzer sounded. Tom removed the muffins and casserole from the oven. As they talked, Cynthia had lost track of the reason she was there and become interested in the man himself.

"What kind of hopes do you have for Ryan's future?" the social worker asked. "Do you want him to go to college, for instance, or would you be just as happy to see him go to vocational school and learn a trade?"

Tom answered swiftly. "I want him to go to college. Education is important."

"What if he isn't bright enough to go to college?"

"There are colleges for people of every ability level and interest. I think I can find a place for him." He paused to ruffle his son's hair. "Although to be perfectly honest, from everything I've observed about Ryan, he seems to be very bright."

"What if he later develops some kind of disability, learning or otherwise?" Irene asked.

Tom gazed fondly at Ryan. "I'd love him no matter what," he said softly.

Cynthia believed him. And so, apparently, did the social worker.

Without warning, the phone rang. He reached behind him for the receiver. "Cynthia, it's for you." He handed the phone across to her.

Cynthia tensed, knowing there was only one person she'd given this number to. "Hi, Mom, what's up?" She hoped nothing was wrong. "Sure, I don't mind bringing your Powell flute and some music over to rehab, but, Mom, are you sure you're ready for this?" Her mother assured her she was.

"Okay, I'll bring it over when I see you tomorrow. Bye."

Tom and the social worker were both looking at her when she hung up, obviously wondering what had her looking so worried. Cynthia explained about Faith's car accident, and subsequent recuperation.

"Is she going to recover completely?" Tom asked, a sympathetic light in his eyes.

"That's just it—we don't know yet." With effort, Cynthia shook off her foreboding thoughts. She sighed. "I just hope it's not too soon for her to be trying to play the flute."

"Maybe it'll help her, having it around. Inspire her," Irene suggested.

"Maybe," Cynthia said.

Tom's dinner was every bit as good as it looked. The four of them gobbled up the nutritious fare and then, at Tom's insistence, left the dishes soaking in the sink and went off to Ryan's carpeted playroom to watch him play.

By the end of the laugh-filled session, Cynthia knew Tom had nothing to worry about—as far as the social worker's evaluation was concerned. With the love and tenderness Tom had shown his son—especially when they were playing together—the report had to be glowing. She was also aware that she knew Tom a lot better now, too.

And she also knew something else—when this all ended, if it ended in such a way that allowed them to be civil to one another in the future, she would like very much to get to know him better. Much better...

Chapter Five

The phone rang while Tom was finishing up the chase scene on the Golden Gate bridge. Satisfied by the way his hero had eluded the hired assassins from the French Mafia, he pushed the save button on his computer and picked up the receiver.

"Have I got some terrific news for you!" Toby Williams chortled.

Tom grinned. "What's up, Toby?" he drawled, stretching and turning off his computer.

"We just sold the movie rights to *Crossbones and Terror* to Universal Studios. They're talking about getting Kathleen Turner for the female lead."

Tom sat up with a jolt, stunned and elated all at once. "That's great!"

He'd considered his book detailing modern-day piracy on the open seas his best work, even before it hit the *New York Times* bestseller list, but he had never imagined this. Not so soon, anyway. He had always figured he'd be old and gray before one of his books made it to the big screen.

"There's a lot of interest in you now and we want to take advantage of it," Toby continued enthusiastically. "Your next book will be out in a few months. And to celebrate, we'd like you to do a publicity tour and really play up your image as a suave, debonair man about town, kind of like the hero in your novels. You'll hit all the night spots, be seen in all the 'in' places. We'll surround you with beautiful women, really play it up—"

What Toby was describing probably would have appealed to Tom when he was in his twenties, but not now, not when he had Ryan to think about. "No," he said firmly.

"What do you mean no? You've done this before!"

"I've done tours," Tom remarked dryly, propping his sneaker-clad feet up on the edge of his desk. "I haven't tried to be 007."

"Yeah, well, you should," Toby argued back. "That James Bond stuff is what makes your writing so exciting. Come on, Tom, it'll be fun. Kind of like old times. Remember when you used to come to New York and we'd paint the town red?"

How could Tom forget? There's been nights at the "21" Club, Elaine's, Maxwell Plum's, and the Hard Rock Café. They'd squired gorgeous women to the hippest comedy clubs, the trendiest discos, even though dancing until dawn had never really been Tom's style.

He still felt he owed Toby a lot, but a publicity tour now—especially the type the editor had in mind—was out of the question. "I appreciate your offering to do this, but I'm going to have to turn you down."

"Tom!"

"My life has changed. I've got a son now." *And a lawsuit pending*.

After a moment of silence, Toby asked, "Well, what about the new series? How are the outlines going? Got anything for me to look at yet?"

"I haven't had time to work on it yet. I've got plenty of ideas, good ones, but the material isn't organized."

"When can I see something?"

"I don't know. Soon." On the intercom speaker of the nursery monitor beside him, Tom heard Ryan stir. He was waking up from his nap. "Look, Toby, I've got to go. I'll talk to you later. And thanks again for the good news."

"Yeah, well, celebrate tonight!"

"I will." Although probably not in the way Toby did. No, Tom would pass on the champagne and women and probably indulge in extra-rich chocolate cake. He laughed and shook his head, thinking about the way his life had changed in the past year.

By the time Tom walked into Ryan's room moments later, his son was sitting up, sleepily looking around. He had his blanket clutched in one hand, his Snoopy in the other.

Tom lifted him up into his arms. Ryan snuggled close and Tom inhaled the sweet baby scent of his skin. His arms tightened around his son, and he felt a wave of love so strong it brought tears to his eyes.

Composing himself, he took Ryan out to the kitchen for some juice. As he settled Ryan into the high chair, there was a rap at the back door. His neighbor, Jasmine Gonzalez, was standing at the door. She was dressed in a halter-style tennis dress that showed off her diminutive figure to perfection. She carried a big stack of photocopied material and several thick manila envelopes in her arms.

"Well, I've got the information on Mission Street you wanted. The Fairmont was nice enough to give us a layout of the whole hotel. And I've got a couple of menus from the most popular restaurants in Chinatown."

"Thanks," Tom said. When he'd first started writing, he'd done all his own research. Since Ryan had come into his life, he'd hired research help. His neighbor had proved a tireless assistant. She and her husband, Frank, were also good friends.

"Heard from Frank lately?" Tom asked. A geologist, Frank traveled frequently and was often gone on assignment for two weeks or more at a time.

"He called last night. He's still in Alaska. He doesn't know when he'll be home."

"How're the boys?" As Tom spoke, he checked on the stew simmering in the Crockpot.

Jasmine rolled her eyes. Her thirteen-year-old twins, Whitney and Wesley, were simultaneously the joy of her life and the bane. "They decided cutting lawns for people was too much work." Determined to be rich, or at least own a closetful of Nintendo games, the boys were always looking for a way to make a buck. "Their latest brainstorm is a dog-sitting service. They've been walking dogs for neighbors who work."

"Sounds reasonable to me." Even though the twins were overly energetic, they were generally responsible and always, always meant well. Dog-walking seemed harmless, and Tom couldn't see why Jasmine was worried.

"I know. Doesn't it, though. But it's these simple ideas of theirs that always end up generating the most trouble. I keep thinking, what can go wrong as long as they keep the dogs on leashes and mind their manners when speaking to the pet owners. But then I think about that car-washing venture they were into a few months ago. At first glance, that sounded harmless, too."

And it had been, Tom knew, until the twins had tried to save money by creating their own car wax. They'd mixed some chemicals they had purchased at a hobby shop. The results had taken part of the finish off an irate owner's car. The price to have the car refinished had cost more than the boys had earned in the two-month venture.

He shook his head, remembering. "I think they learned their lesson the last time."

"Right." Jasmine rolled her eyes. "No more experiments with the chemistry set."

"I'm sure it will be fine," Tom soothed.

Jasmine looked as if she didn't agree, but grinned, appreciating this verbal support. "So how are you?" she asked. "I know you had your session with the social worker and Ryan's guardian last night."

"It went okay," Tom said.

"Just okay?" Jasmine frowned, able to read his moods with lightning swiftness.

Tom knew if there was anyone he could confide in outside his family, it was Jasmine. "It's weird," he admitted. "I feel like I can't be myself when I'm around them. I'm wary of every word I say." He swallowed hard. "And that Cynthia Whittiker, I feel like she's judging me every second. Which of course she is."

"It's her job," Jasmine pointed out levelly.

"I know." Tom sighed. "I just wish it weren't." Because last night, for a few short moments when they'd lapsed into casual conversation, he had seen what it could be like had they not been embroiled in this custody suit. He knew, under other circumstances, that he and Cynthia had the potential to be . . . friends?

But now, as things were, she just felt like an unwelcome authority figure in his life. And that bothered him, too. He didn't like relying on other people's opinion of him for his success. He'd always made his own way. He'd always been unerringly successful. Until now.

"Got another session with her tonight?" Jasmine asked.

"Yeah, she'll be here. But it's Sally Ann's turn to spend time with Ryan and the social worker."

"How come they're not doing that at her house?"

"Ryan doesn't know her well enough. They think he'll warm up to her faster if he's in a familiar environment."

"Oh. Makes sense."

"Anyway, the social worker will visit Sally Ann in her home environment in a separate visit."

"Well, if it gets to be too much for you, having all that going on at your house tonight and you want to get out for a while, let me know. I'm going out to play tennis in a few minutes, but I'll be home after that."

"Thanks," Tom said, "but I think I'll stick around."

"Still don't trust Sally Ann, do you?"

Tom shook his head grimly. "Not one whit." As Jasmine got up to go, he remembered he hadn't paid her for the work she'd done. He wrote her a check, and then, with Ryan in his arms, walked her to the door.

On impulse, Jasmine said, "It'll be all right, Tom, really," and then to reinforce her words, gave him a reassuring peck on the cheek. And it was precisely then that Cynthia Whittiker pulled her car into his drive. There could be no doubt she had seen the kiss, and also no doubt that she had misinterpreted it. It was all Tom could do not to groan out loud.

Jasmine said under her breath, "Guess I better stick around long enough for you to set her straight, hmm?"

Tom nodded. "If you don't mind."

"My neighbor, Jasmine Gonzalez," he said to Cynthia, when she got within earshot. To his relief, Cynthia accepted the introduction pleasantly. As a result the two women chatted amiably for a minute before Jasmine went on home.

"She's a close friend, I gather?" Cynthia asked as Tom escorted her into his home.

There it was, what he'd been expecting—the faint undertone of suspicion. He held her gaze candidly. Although it was the end of the workday, her golden skin glowed with vitality. He tried hard not to notice how soft and kissable her lips looked with their soft sheen of gloss.

"Jasmine and I are very close friends. She and her husband, Frank, both are," he said.

As he had hoped, Cynthia got the message, but seconds later as the two of them waited for Sally Ann and the social worker to arrive, he became excruciatingly aware that the incident had opened up a whole new area, one they hadn't begun to discuss.

"Well, as long as we seem to have a few minutes I guess I might as well find out a little more about you for my report to Judge Mitchum. Unless you object?"

"No." Tom sat down next to Ryan, playing with a stack of blocks on the floor. Although it would be nice to have a normal conversation once, he thought, just the two of them, but he supposed that was impossible under the circumstances.

Cynthia took a seat on the sofa. He watched her cross her legs at the knee, uncomfortably aware of the flash of dark silky stockings on slim thighs he saw beneath her trim black skirt. He wondered about the rest of her.

As soon as the thought entered his mind, he knew he had to get rid of it. This wasn't a character in one of his books, nor someone he could fantasize about. He forced his glance up. It didn't get much easier. Above her trim waist was the soft press of her full breasts against her red silk blouse. As his glance slid higher, he saw the gleaming curtain of her hair brushing her slim shoulders, the soft parted lips open over straight white teeth, the frank hazel eyes with the long gold-tipped lashes.

Whether he wanted to admit it to himself or not, he thought, the lady was enticing, beautiful, sexy. Just looking at her inspired a wealth of fantasies. And though he would've liked to chalk it all up to the writer in him, he knew he couldn't. He'd seen plenty of beautiful women in his time, but not one of them had ever had this effect on him.

"So, how's your social life?" Cynthia asked briskly, taking out her notepad and pen. "I know you mentioned earlier, in one of our talks, that you didn't get out much, but are you dating anyone special?"

Just the fact she had a right to ask him a question like that made him feel invaded. But what else could she do? He kept his voice soft. "Since Ryan was born, I've had very few dates."

"Then you're not seeing anyone in particular now?"

"No."

"Do you miss dating more regularly?" Cynthia continued, making a few more notes.

He smiled, perversely pleased at the depth of her interest. "Sometimes," he confided.

Cynthia gave him an intense look, as if she were wondering if he was being totally honest with her, and then bent her head slightly as she wrote, again avoiding his eyes. Without wanting to, he inhaled the fresh flowery scent of her hair and skin. She was very appealing, very feminine. He couldn't help but wonder wryly where she'd been when he'd been out actively looking for a potential wife. Because if he'd met someone like her then, he might never have gotten into this situation in the first place. He would have spent his time chasing her, instead of finding and hiring a surrogate.

"What do you do when that happens?" she asked, looking up.

"When what happens?" Tom asked, panicking a little because he'd totally lost track of the conversation.

She gave him a strange look. "When you realize you miss dating?"

He spread his hands, then smiled when Ryan, seeing the opportunity for a hug, tumbled into his arms. "Generally, I call up some friends and we go out to dinner in a group." He pressed a kiss into Ryan's hair. Ryan toddled back over to his plastic building blocks. He plopped down on the floor beside them.

"What about you?" Tom turned back to Cynthia curiously. "Seeing anyone?"

He'd meant only to goad her a little and hence get out of an area of discussion so intensely personal. Her lips parted in silent protest, but for a second she didn't speak at all. "No, I'm not," she said finally, in a perplexed tone.

He wasn't sure why she had answered him—after all, this third degree was supposed to be for him—but now that she had, he found he wanted to know more about her. He couldn't imagine anyone as beautiful and smart as Cynthia not being booked up for weeks. "Why not?" he asked softly.

"Why not you?" she tossed back flirtatiously.

Her smile made him feel reckless. "I don't go out that much anymore because somewhere in the past couple of years I got beyond the point of going out with someone, anyone, just to be going out." He knew from the sudden glimmer in her eyes that she understood. Pleased, he said candidly, "I'd rather be single, and spend time with my family and married friends, than be out with someone I know isn't right for me."

"I know what you mean," she acknowledged quietly. She sighed, and for a moment ignored her notebook and pen. "Lately, I've felt that way, too." Her voice dropped a husky notch, until it was as rich and mellow as aged whiskey. "But sometimes I wonder if it isn't hopelessly naive of me to just sit around and wait for something magical to happen. But at the same time I'm really tired of trying to conjure up a romance, just for the sake of having a romance. Do you know what I mean?"

Tom knew exactly what she meant. He was surprised and touched they had that in common.

The phone rang. Reluctantly, he excused himself and got up to answer it. Sally Ann was on the line, asking for Cynthia. She took the receiver from him, her hand lightly brushing his in the process, and listened intently for several minutes. She seemed to grow unhappier with every second that passed, but her voice was calm and accepting when she spoke, "All right. No, I understand, Sally Ann. Yes, tomorrow would be fine. I'll try to catch the social worker, but I imagine since her office is across town that she's already left and is on her way here. All right. Yes, see you then."

"Trouble?" Tom asked as Cynthia hung up the phone.

She nodded. "Sally Ann's been called to work a double shift at the hospital. They're shorthanded and she has no choice but to stay. She'll have to reschedule the session with Irene, hopefully for tomorrow. I told her it was all right with me. How do you feel about that?"

Ticked off, Tom thought. "I wonder how often this happens?" he murmured.

Cynthia shrugged, not wanting to get into a discussion of Sally Ann with him. "Will this be taken into consideration when custody is decided, the fact that Sally Ann's work hours can sometimes be long and unpredictable?"

To his frustration, Cynthia assumed a detached, professional air. "I'm sure it will be noted, along with the comparative flexibility of your job." She paused. "But that doesn't mean you'll get custody of Ryan. The judge will have to look at everything before he makes a decision."

Tom noted that her guard was up again. The confidences and closeness they had just shared were forgotten. Without warning, he was filled with despair. Was this how it was going to be for the next two months? With Cynthia nice to him—almost sympathetic to his plight—one moment, cool and detached the next, in essence telling him he just had to sit back and take whatever was dished out to him and not protest? It seemed so.

The final custody hearing on April twelfth had never seemed so far away.

CYNTHIA HEARD THE SOUNDS of her mother's flute as she walked toward her room. A smile lit her face as she recognized the beautiful tone of the sustained note, but her smile faded as she heard Faith begin to climb the notes of the scale.

Faith sounded worse than a beginner as she struggled to get from note to note. She was having trouble keeping her fingers pressed on the keys.

Cynthia took a deep breath and entered the room. "Hi, Mom—" She stopped as she saw the tears of frustration in her mother's eyes.

Faith put the flute aside with trembling fingers and sat down on the edge of her bed. "It's no use, Cynthia," she said. "I'm never going to be able to play again." Holding out her right hand, she tried vainly to flex her fingers. "I'm going to have to retire."

Cynthia knew that her mom was talking about more than retiring; she was talking about giving up. "Mom, you can't quit!"

"I don't see that I have a choice!"

Cynthia swallowed, trying to get a better grip on her own soaring emotions. What her mother needed now was support. "What did the doctor say?" she asked as calmly as she was able.

"He thinks I'll get better," her mother reported numbly. "But he says I'll never have the mobility I had. And without that, I can't play without sounding as if I'm totally incompetent. Darn it all, Cynthia, I still have it in here!" She thumped the area over her heart. Tears rolled down her face. "It's killing me to not be able to play."

Cynthia knew how much her mother relied on her music. It provided solace, a place to escape to, a place in which she could vent her emotions. It had been her life's work. And now it was beginning to collapse. It wasn't fair, Cynthia thought. It wasn't right this should happen to her mother of all people, who'd never in her entire life done anything to hurt anyone.

For her mother's sake, Cynthia tried to be calm. "Mom, maybe you're just trying to move too fast," she said, gulping back her own tears. "Maybe...maybe if you relaxed more and eased into playing again, instead of trying to regain total dexterity in every finger all at once, you'd have more success."

Faith shook her head sadly. "I've had several months to recover. No, I'm afraid this is one time when I won't be as good as new." She sighed heavily and began disassembling her flute and putting it back in its case.

"What are you going to do?" Cynthia asked, almost afraid to hear the answer.

Her mother's voice was ragged with despair. "Well, I guess the first thing is to end my temporary leave of absence and officially retire." Faith snapped the case shut with a decisive thud, then zipped it into its cloth cover.

"Mom, surely you can't mean that!"

Faith sighed. "I have to be sensible. Yes, the university might be willing to keep me on in some capacity, as a lecturer for instance, but the students in music performance need someone who can demonstrate each technique. They'll have to hire someone new, and the sooner the better. By getting out of the way swiftly, I'll clear the way for the new teacher."

Cynthia watched as her mother got out a paper and pen and began clumsily drafting a resignation letter. Although Cynthia wanted to snatch the paper away from her, she knew one of them had to behave rationally. "Mom, I think you're jumping the gun here," she said evenly.

Faith looked up sadly. "I wish that were so, darling—you don't know how much. But it isn't and I have to face the truth." Her head bent, Faith continued writing in the same illegible scrawl.

Cynthia watched miserably. She knew from experience there was nothing she could say or do to change her mother's mind. Faith would do what she felt she had to do, and as much as Cynthia hated to admit it, a part of her knew her mother was right. Maybe the demands of her university job were too much—even at a distance. Maybe the pressure was hampering her recovery. Perhaps not having that burden on her would speed her recovery, she reasoned slowly. Cynthia sighed. Maybe they both needed a dose of Tom Harrigan's will to succeed; his unabashed self-confidence. She was certainly becoming an appreciator.

"THE OUTLINES LOOK GOOD, Tom, but I need a lot more."

"I figured as much," Tom said, shifting a cranky Ryan to his other hip. He hadn't expected Toby to drop in today, but worried about the lack of progress on his proposed five-book series, Toby had come to Dallas in person. They'd been working together for the past four hours, going over Tom's notes and ideas.

When the doorbell sounded it was all Tom could do not to groan.

Toby said, "I've got a few more notes to make. I'll be back in your office if you need me."

Tom went to the door. "Cynthia, hi," he said. Of all the worst times to come over, he thought, this was it. The place was a mess, and Ryan had yet to be fed.

"May I come in?" Cynthia said, shooting Ryan a concerned look. "I have something I need to talk to you about."

It didn't sound good. "Sure. Just let me tell Toby you're here."

"Toby?"

"My editor. We've been working today."

"No need to come and get me, Tom. I'm on my way out." Toby smiled at Cynthia winningly as Tom introduced her, then said, "I left my suggestions for the series written on that notepad on your desk, Tom. I really need all five outlines by next Friday at the latest. Now, about the publicity tour—"

"Two weeks is too long for me to be gone from Ryan."

"So, take him with you." Toby shrugged. "You can afford to hire a nanny."

"Ten cities in as many days?"

"Tom, we need you to do this. You're hot now." Toby let his voice drop persuasively. "Don't you remember how much fun we used to have when you came to New York? The whole tour could be like that—"

Cynthia's eyes lit up curiously. "Like what?" she said.

"Busy," Tom said, furious at Toby. All he needed was for Cynthia to find out about his previous jaunts in New York with Toby. He rushed to show Toby, who had a plane to catch, out. "I'll think about it, Toby, and get back to you."

Ryan was fussing as Tom shut the door. "I've really got to feed Ryan. Come on into the kitchen with me."

He settled Ryan in his high chair, then got three jars of baby food from the cupboard. He thought he saw disapproval in Cynthia's eyes, although she was working hard to veil her feelings. "You said you wanted to talk to me," he said.

She nodded. Reaching into her purse, she pulled out a slim white envelope. "Sally Ann asked me to give you this."

Worried by her solemn look, Tom took the envelope. Inside was a cashier's check made out to him for ten thousand dollars. "She's returning the surrogate fee," he said slowly, staring at the check in shock.

As if that simple action on her part would negate everything, including her short-lived promises. She'd be absolved now for trying to destroy his life with his son.

Fighting hard to keep a handle on his feelings, Tom sat down to feed Ryan. "Did you know about this?" he said levelly.

"No." She gave him a hard, discerning look. "Not until after it was done."

Silence fell between them. Aware his every word was now being judged, Tom fed his son carefully and gently, not speaking again until his temper was under control.

"I didn't think she had this kind of money," he said finally.

"She doesn't," Cynthia replied. "She sold her car."

That sounded like Sally Ann's strategy, Tom couldn't help but think mean-spiritedly. "How's she going to get around?"

"I don't know. I asked her the same thing. She said something about using the bus or getting rides from friends until she can secure a loan for another car."

She paused, raking her teeth over her lower lip again. "Does it bother you that Sally Ann paid you back?"

Although Tom was trying very hard to appear relaxed, he was aware his voice was brusque when he answered honestly, "In a way. I preferred it when everything was nice and legal, spelled out in that contract she signed."

She moved forward urgently, both her elbows on the table. "That contract the two of you signed was never worth the paper it was written on. Surrogate parenting agreements are invalid and unenforceable under current law."

Ryan spit out his last spoonful, his signal he was finished. Tom lifted him from the high chair and countered, "And yet they are still being written."

"With less frequency. But you're right. Sometimes invalid or not, the contracts work." She followed him back into the hall and down to Ryan's bedroom.

Tom sighed as he began putting Ryan into his pajamas. "Thanks for bringing the check by."

"No problem. I thought it would be easier."

It had been. But he didn't want to think about it anymore. He didn't want to talk about Sally Ann. "If that's all, though, I've really got to put Ryan to bed."

"Actually, it isn't," Cynthia said, surprising him. "I need to talk to you about your work. About some things that Toby said. But if you're too busy, I can talk to you another time."

The pretty lawyer's worried about what she'd seen here tonight. I can't let her leave thinking I'm this disorganized, pressured all the time. "No, that'll be fine, but let's go into the living room." He supposed he could wait to change Ryan and rock him to sleep.

Tom took a seat in a cushioned rocker. Cynthia sat on the sofa. "Does this count as a spot check?" Tom asked.

Cynthia gave him a half smile. "It seems to be turning into one, doesn't it?"

Yes. And he didn't like the way it was going so far.

"About book tours," Cynthia began. "Are you going to be able to refuse them?"

She doesn't pull any punches. His temper, never very easily contained, had been taxed to the boiling point. "Yes."

She looked skeptical. "Your editor won't pressure you?"

"He'll pressure me. I won't give in." He noted she still looked unconvinced. With a sigh, he explained, "I'm not interested in being a celebrity. I just want to write my books, have them read." He bent and put Ryan down on the floor, messy with toys, Tom noted ruefully. He wondered how many demerits that would get him.

"Is that because you grew up in a famous household?" Cynthia pressed.

"I hadn't really thought about it, but yeah, I guess it is." He paused, then because she was looking so genuinely interested, he went on softly, "I know what it is to grow up under the constant scrutiny and pressures of the limelight. We dealt with it in our house by keeping the lowest profile possible. That's why I write under a pen name. I want my private life to be private, not fodder for scandal magazines.''

"Did you do a lot of publicity tours before Ryan was born?"

She's wondering about the fun Toby was hinting at, Tom thought. *She's wondering why I shut him up.*

Cynthia took a pen and notepad from her purse. Tom's eyes narrowed. He resented that they couldn't have a conversation without her recording it. But he quickly pushed the emotion away, realizing that this was her job—to evaluate his performance as a parent. He ought to feel grateful she was determined to do it so thoroughly; after all, it meant Sally Ann was getting the same treatment. And after the grandstanding effort to pay back the surrogate fee, he felt her actions bore close examination, too.

Mindful of her unanswered question, he said, "Before Ryan was born, I went on tour whenever they asked. I had no reason not to."

Before they could continue, the phone rang. Tom shook his head, unable to mask his exasperation. "This seems to be my night for interruptions."

No sooner had he said hello, than he began to smile. "You've got the movie? Great. I'll be right over to—" Suddenly remembering Cynthia's presence, he stopped and cast her a glance. "Can you hold it for me until eight or eight-thirty?"

Unfortunately that was against the rules. "No, I understand," he said. "I'll be right over to get it." He hung up and turned to Cynthia. "I've got to run over to the video store to pick up a tape I reserved. Why don't you ride over with me and Ryan? We could talk along the way."

For a moment, Cynthia hesitated. "Sure," she said finally. *It might be good to see how Ryan behaves when in a store, with other children,* she thought. "What movie is it?" she asked, after they'd all gotten in the car and he had buckled Ryan in securely.

Tom put on his own seat belt, then started the Bronco. "*Bull Durham*, my all-time favorite baseball movie." He backed out of the drive and into the street. "I saw the picture in the theaters, but never got around to seeing it on videotape. It's never in the store when I go, so I asked them to reserve it for me."

"I liked that movie, too," Cynthia said.

To Tom's relief, despite the fact that it was past his bedtime, Ryan was perfectly behaved during the errand. By the time they returned to the house, he was getting sleepy. Tom whisked him off for a quick diaper change, and then as had been his practice since he'd weaned Ryan from the bottle a few weeks earlier, he took him out to the kitchen for a quarter cup of milk. Ryan yawned between practically every sip. "He didn't get much of a nap today."

Cynthia gazed fondly down at Ryan. "He does look tired," she commented softly, not seeming in such a big hurry to get on with the questions anymore. Tom was glad she'd unbent a little.

Back in the living room, Tom put the movie on and sat down in the rocker. "Since I weaned Ryan from his

bottle on the advice of his pediatrician, I've rocked him
to sleep watching television.''

"He won't fall asleep when you read to him?''

"Generally no.'' Tom smiled. "He gets too busy
helping me turn the pages. At the moment, television
is the only thing that works.'' As had become custom-
ary, Tom situated Ryan so his head was cradled on his
shoulder, facing the television.

Cynthia, seeing Ryan start to settle down again and
fall asleep, picked up where they had left off. For the
next twenty or thirty minutes, they whispered back and
forth in hushed tones while Cynthia talked to Tom
about the demands of his work in general and Toby in
particular. She seemed concerned.

Tom did his best to reassure her, and he thought he
succeeded, despite the distraction of the movie they
surreptitiously watched as they talked. About halfway
through, they stopped talking and just enjoyed it.

It was almost over when Tom realized there was
really no reason for him to still be rocking Ryan. Getting up, he padded noiselessly to the rear of the house.
He returned moments later, reporting happily, "Out
like a light.''

Cynthia smiled. When the credits rolled later, Tom
was surprised to see that Cynthia had tears in her eyes.
He had never guessed her feelings about a big screen
love story could run so deep. Knowing that intrigued
him. It made him aware she was, under all the sophisticated clothing and professionalism, a woman with a
lot of heart. A woman he yearned to know better.

An embarrassed look on her face, she got up to go. Figuring she didn't want him to comment on her uncommonly emotional mood, Tom walked her wordlessly to the door and leaned one shoulder against the frame as she stepped outside. "Thanks for staying tonight," he said sincerely. "After the day I had, I needed to kick back."

She seemed to understand instinctively how much stress he was under. Her hazel eyes darkened sympathetically, and she tucked an errant strand of hair behind her ear. He tracked the sensual movement, aware his mouth and throat suddenly felt parched and tight.

"Thanks for letting me watch the movie," she said, answering him in the same, almost too casual tone.

He nodded and thought, *I want to kiss her. I want to say to hell with everything and just pull her into my arms and kiss her until she surrenders. I want to feel the softness of her mouth under mine, discover her sweetness and her strength and her taste. Only I can't do that, can't even let myself think about it, because of Ryan and the custody case.* His hands tightened into fists at his sides and he sighed. If there were an award for being in the wrong place at the wrong time, he would win it hands down.

For the first time in his life he had found a woman who was utterly intriguing. Beguiling. Bewitching and bewildering. If she was thinking the same about him, though, wanting him in the same way he wanted her, he had no clue. She seemed only to hold him at arm's length.

She smiled uncertainly at him. Feeling the need to reassure her, he smiled back. He couldn't help but wish that it hadn't been the custody case that had brought them together. But maybe when all this business was over....

Chapter Six

Funny, Cynthia thought, ringing the bell for the fifth time. Tom always answered the door promptly. And he'd known she was coming to supervise one of Ryan's thrice-weekly visitations with his mother.

Of course she couldn't blame him if he was avoiding her after the silly way she'd acted during the movie. She couldn't even explain it herself. She just knew that, sitting there with Tom and Ryan, she'd become aware of how much was missing in her life. How time was passing her by and she was no closer to her dream of marriage and family than she'd been when she was twenty. And for the first time she had realized how Tom might have felt when he'd made the decision to hire a surrogate. For the first time she had empathized with him completely. And that worried her, because she didn't want to lose her objectivity.

Frustrated with the lack of response from inside the house, she moved across the porch to the front window and peered in. His house looked deserted.

From the rear of the house, however, she could hear activity—voices and occasional bursts of laughter.

Going around to the back yard, she saw Tom and two teenage boys who looked like identical versions of Dennis the Menace, with their white blond hair and matching cowlicks, and a bevy of damp golden retriever puppies. All three guys were soaked and surrounded by puddles of water. Several empty containers of dog shampoo were scattered on the ground.

Tom looked up at her approach. His face registered shock then dismay. He seemed to have totally forgotten she was coming. "Uh, Ryan's not here," Tom said, as he wiped a stray bit of suds still clinging to his face.

The two boys gave Cynthia a curious look, then began snapping leashes on the puppies. With a "Thanks for helping us, Tom!" they headed for the gate with the dogs.

"Anytime, Whitney," Tom said pleasantly, walking over to turn off the hose.

"Want us to tell Mom to bring Ryan back over now?" the other asked, as he held open the gate.

"Yeah, that would be great."

Promising to do as Tom requested, the boys left.

Seeming to be in no great hurry to set the disaster zone to rights, Tom casually rewound the garden hose and began picking up the empty shampoo bottles. Jasmine dropped off Ryan with a quick hello to Cynthia and Tom. At that moment they could hear the doorbell ring.

"That must be Sally Ann," Cynthia said as they went inside. It was her night with Ryan.

Tom's face took on a grim, unreadable look. "I've got work to do," he said, handing Ryan over to Cynthia. "If you need me, I'll be in my office."

Trying not to let Tom's curtness get to her, she went to let Sally Ann in, wishing for Ryan's sake that Tom were better able to handle the entrance of his son's mother into their lives.

"Hi!" Sally Ann seemed chipper.

Ryan squealed in delight and held out his arms for a hug. Sally Ann laughed and held him close. Together, they went back to the playroom where Ryan's toys were kept.

"Ball," Ryan said, giving a bright blue ball to his mother.

"Very good, Ryan!" Sally Ann beamed as she accepted his present.

Soon a baby-level game of catch ensued. Watching, Cynthia noted the progress they had made. Sally Ann had a knack with kids.

When the session was over, Cynthia took Ryan to Tom's office, then walked Sally Ann to the door. "You're doing very well with Ryan," she remarked.

"I think I'm good for him," Sally Ann replied fiercely. She looked at Cynthia, her expression determined, almost daring Ryan's guardian to try to deny it. "In fact, I know I am."

Cynthia glanced at her kindly. "I know you are, too, Sally Ann."

"Tom doesn't," Sally Ann responded bitterly. "Have you seen how he looks at me whenever I'm around, like I'm an intruder in Ryan's life, like I have no right to be with him at all?"

Yes, Cynthia had noticed it. She had also noticed Tom was going out of his way lately to avoid conflict with her. He disappeared into his office the moment he knew she was around, and didn't come out until she'd left.

"I mean, it's not as if I planned this," Sally Ann continued vehemently. "As if I wanted to ruin Tom's life." She let out an anguished breath. "I never expected to have the feelings I have for Ryan! I thought I'd be able to forget him, to have children of my own someday. But now I can't." The tears she'd been holding back spilled over her cheeks. She leaned against the doorjamb for support.

"I understand, Sally Ann. I do."

Sally Ann looked at her, trying to determine if that was true. Finally she nodded, then said in more subdued tones, "Tom's lawyer told mine that he thinks it's just my sterility driving me, that if it weren't for that, I never would have come to claim him."

Cynthia smiled.

Sally Ann's light blue eyes softened. "I think that's a small part of it. Maybe if I could have a baby of my own now, I would feel differently about wanting Ryan. But all that's beside the point, isn't it? Since I can't have a baby, and he *is* my son." She paused again, looking as if she were about to burst into tears again. "He needs me, can't you see that?"

Cynthia knew Sally Ann needed Ryan. She also knew Ryan liked Sally Ann and enjoyed being with her. But need? She wondered if Sally Ann was able to separate her needs from the needs of her child.

Sally Ann sighed and continued, "That day in the hospital, when I saw him, I realized for the first time that he wasn't just Tom's son—he was mine, too." Her voice choked up. "I realized then how much I had missed, by not being part of his first year of life. And I wanted to make it up to him.''

There was no doubt the two of them had forged a closeness, Cynthia thought. They would see what happened in the future.

WHEN CYNTHIA WENT BACK to tell Tom she was leaving, he was in Ryan's bedroom. And the look on his face was frantic.

"Cynthia, come here. Look at this," he said.

She peered over his shoulder. A red rash ran from Ryan's tummy, over his arms and shoulders, and down his legs to his feet.

"Does he have a fever?" she asked, concerned, noting Tom had already begun taking his son's temperature. There was a recent outbreak of measles in Texas.

"I don't know. He doesn't feel hot to me, but you can't always tell that way," Tom said, still holding a thermometer between Ryan's arm and his chest. "We'll know in a minute."

"Has he been vaccinated for measles?" she asked, making funny faces at Ryan. Faces Ryan made right back at her.

"No, not yet. They don't get their MMR shot until they're fifteen months old now. They've found it isn't really effective until then."

Oh, no, Cynthia thought, dread filling her. *Please, don't let Ryan get anything as potentially serious as measles.*

Removing the thermometer from under Ryan's arm, Tom frowned and said, "Well, his temperature's normal."

Nonetheless, the rash was worrisome. Cynthia wished Sally Ann were still there; they could have used her medical expertise. She bit her lower lip anxiously. "Have you called his pediatrician?"

"If you'll watch Ryan, I'll do it now."

He came back minutes later, looking even more disgruntled. "His doctor's out to dinner," Tom reported unhappily, getting some clean clothing out of Ryan's dresser. "His answering service suggested I take Ryan to the emergency room. The rash should be looked at." Tom sat down in the rocking chair and began quickly dressing Ryan. Although he was acting very calm, Cynthia could see he was upset. She didn't feel a crisis like this was anything he—or anyone else—should have to go through alone.

"I'll go with you," she volunteered, telling herself that as Ryan's court-appointed legal guardian, she needed to be there, too.

To Cynthia's and Tom's relief, Ryan was fine on the drive over. Once in the emergency room, however, he became very fussy. He rubbed at his face and arms, trying to scratch the rash that seemed to get more inflamed by the minute. He cried when the doctor tried to examine him.

Later, the doctor spoke to both Tom and Cynthia. "It isn't the measles. It's contact dermatitis. What's Ryan been around lately that's different? Do you have any new carpeting, new clothes maybe that haven't been washed?"

"No, but I recently switched laundry detergents," Tom said thoughtfully. "Do you think that could be it?"

"More than likely," the doctor said. "I suggest you return to your original detergent. In the meantime, I'm going to prescribe an ointment for Ryan, and a few doses of oral antihistamine. You can bathe him in baking soda and water, too—it'll help cut down on the itching."

Tom thanked the doctor, and with Cynthia's help, dressed his son. "We're going to have to stop at the pharmacy on the way home," Tom said, consulting his watch.

Cynthia didn't mind. "I can help as long as you need me to," she told him.

He sent her a shy smile of gratitude. "Thanks."

The moment strung out intimately. Cynthia wanted to tell him it was nothing, but she couldn't find the words. He, too, seemed not to know what to say.

They barely made it in before the drugstore closed at nine. Once in the car again, Ryan was yawning and slightly grumpy again. "Poor kid, he's exhausted," Tom said softly.

His daddy looked exhausted, too, Cynthia couldn't help but note. Thinking back to all that had happened just since she had arrived at his home at five-thirty, Cynthia realized it was no wonder. "I can stay a little longer, if you need me." As Ryan's guardian, she told herself firmly, it was her duty.

"Thanks," Tom said. "I'd appreciate it if you would. I'm going to have to hunt down something for him to wear that hasn't been washed in the new detergent."

"What about the sheets on his bed?"

"They're okay, thank goodness."

Once inside his house again, they bathed Ryan and put him to bed.

Afterward, Cynthia looked around for her belongings, her heart light and happy from their evening's sharing. Tom followed her, a genial look on his face. "Thanks for helping me out tonight," he said in the hushed silence of the house. For a moment his eyes met hers and held, transmitting a need that went far past anything required by his son. A jolt of awareness went through her. Heat shimmered through her, rendering her motionless, and he seemed similarly entranced.

Tom cleared his throat and said, "I would have managed without you, of course, but it would've been a lot harder."

For the first time she had a sense of what an incredible responsibility he had taken on alone. Feeling suddenly shy, and wary of the crazy jolts of emotion she felt, she ducked her head. "You're welcome," she said finally, her throat feeling unaccountably dry while her palms were wet. "I'm just glad he's okay."

"So am I," Tom said, his relief evident.

Silence fell between them again, and this time the tension between them was almost overpowering. His eyes held hers, asking, wanting, much more than she could give. She was supposed to remain emotionally detached here, impartial, but at the moment, looking into Tom's eyes, she felt anything but. She could fall for this man, and his son, in a very major way. She could easily become a part of their tightly knit unit—by default. And that wouldn't do at all, because once this case was settled, there would be no room for her in Tom's life. For him even to see her then might prove to be only an unpleasant reminder of this tumultuous time in his life.

Chastened, Cynthia said finally, "I've got to go." In a state of panic and confusion, with unaccustomed cowardice, she fled. As she had expected, as the formality of the situation demanded, Tom didn't try to stop her. She was left feeling oddly and inappropriately disappointed.

Chapter Seven

Tom walked out of the psychologist's office feeling emotionally exhausted. The truth was he hated everything about these visits. For now, he not only had to see the court-appointed psychologist Cynthia had selected, but the experts his own lawyer had chosen to testify on his behalf, as well.

They'd start with questions about his upbringing, his life before Ryan, his decision to have a child via surrogacy. And then they'd get into the details of his life today, how he felt about writing, how difficult it was to raise a child alone, his feelings about Sally Ann now.

And those were the questions that bothered him the most.

He couldn't lie, couldn't say he welcomed her intrusion. Couldn't express the depth of his resentment and anger toward her.

He sighed, wishing there were an easy solution. His steps picked up as he left the medical building and crossed the parking lot toward his Bronco.

"Mr. Harrigan? Mr. Tom Harrigan, or should I say, Harrison James?"

The voice seemed to come out of nowhere. Tom turned around, found himself confronted with a guy in a rumpled white suit and long-sleeved blue silk shirt. Pulling a wallet from his pocket, he opened it and flashed a press badge. "Sam Reeb, from *Personalities* magazine. We got wind of this custody case you're embroiled in. We thought you might like to tell us your side of the story, get the word out to all your fans what's happening in your life. After all, this is pretty interesting stuff—single father being sued by the child's mother. Might sell a lot of books." Then, as if he had every right to ask, "What was your relationship with Sally Ann Anderson, anyway?"

Tom's blood chilled. No way would he let his son be used for fodder between magazine pages. Bad enough they were intruding in his private life, but to try to ruin Ryan's! "I don't know what you're talking about," he retorted with an inner calm he didn't feel.

"Come on, Mr. Harrigan." Sam Reeb's eyes darkened threateningly. "Don't fence with me. I have it from good authority that a Ms. Sally Ann Anderson is suing you for custody of your son."

So Reeb knew about Sally Ann, too, Tom thought, having to work to hide his dismay. Did Reeb know about the surrogacy contract?

Tom had an impulse to deck the guy on the spot. With effort, he checked it. "Look, you're way off track," Tom said curtly, thinking, dammit, how did any of this get out? And if Reeb didn't know about the surrogacy contract, how long could they keep it secret? If Sally Ann or Cynthia had told someone...

"I don't think I am," the tenacious reporter insisted smugly. "I think something is going on here." He waited for Tom to say something. When he didn't reply, he said, "I'm gonna find out the whole story, you know. All about your failed romance with Sally Ann and why she initially gave the baby over to you to raise, everything. It's only a matter of time."

Tom kept his face expressionless. This was just like a poker game, he told himself sternly, only the stakes were a lot higher. A boy's future, his right to privacy.

"Do what you want," he told the reporter, then with a dangerous look, he added, "But watch what you print. If so much as one word of it is untrue, I'll sue you and your publisher for libel."

Sam turned away with an indifferent shrug, showing how callous he really was. "If you change your mind and want to talk," he called casually over his shoulder, "I'm staying at the Airport Marriott."

Tom got into the Bronco, drove to the nearest pay phone and called Sally Ann at the hospital.

Swiftly, he told her about the reporter from *Personalities*. Sally Ann confirmed the reporter hadn't been there yet.

Tom felt relief. "Well, he's probably on his way. Don't tell him anything, Sally Ann. Not anything! Right now he's just fishing. If we keep quiet, he won't have a thing to print."

"Well, of course I won't talk to him," she said, sounding indignant. "You know what the judge said. The records in this case are sealed."

"And they have to stay that way," Tom repeated firmly, "so remember if you have a choice, don't see Sam Reeb at all."

"I won't, I promise," she said.

Feeling a little better, Tom said goodbye and hung up the phone. Then he headed straight for Cynthia's office. Ignoring her secretary's admonition that she was on the phone, he barged into her office. Her brows rose, but she shook her head at her secretary and waved her away, indicating it was okay, she could handle Tom.

Her eyes still on him, Cynthia swiftly wrapped up her business. Hanging up the phone, she said, "What's wrong?"

"I just finished talking to a guy from *Personalities* magazine. He'd heard I was involved in a custody battle. Sally Ann says it wasn't her who leaked the story, and I have to believe her because he seemed to know nothing about the surrogacy arrangement. But someone's talking and I want to know who."

"Unfortunately, Tom, lots of people know about it. The lawyers, their staffs, the courts, the psychologists and counselors we've hired to evaluate the three of you..."

"But they were all sworn to secrecy!"

"Well, obviously someone somewhere broke that vow." She frowned, then pushed her chair away from her desk and drummed her fingers on the polished wooden surface. "Finding out where the leak came from may prove a little harder. What'd you say this reporter's name was?"

Tom gave it, and the hotel where he was staying.

Cynthia fell silent. When she finally spoke, he could tell he had her complete and utter sympathy. "What are you going to do?"

"I don't know," he said, his voice brusque. "I guess I call my lawyer and we talk to the judge. Beyond that, I don't know." He shrugged, not remembering when he'd ever felt so helpless. He wondered if and when it would ever end. And if he'd be able to bring Ryan and himself out of it unscathed.

Out loud, he continued, "If we go to Sam Reeb and lean on him, he'll know for sure something is up."

"Which would only make him all the more curious."

"Right." Tom felt bitterness invade his soul. "So I guess that leaves us only one alternative—remain quiet for the time being." It felt like a ridiculously impotent solution to a pressing problem, but Tom didn't know what else to do. One thing for sure, he couldn't let his frustration lead him to do anything rash. Although he had the feeling that was just what Sam Reeb was hoping.

"Looks like we might have to do just that," Cynthia agreed softly, looking suddenly just as worried as he was about the whole situation. "Listen, Tom, you may not believe it now, but it's been my experience that even the worst situations have a way of working out, if we just give them time."

Suddenly he realized how different they were, and he felt aggrieved. She tended to go with the flow, not battle a situation for an outcome beneficial to her. He, on the other hand, had always been a person who went after what he wanted with no holds barred, and he wasn't going to stop now.

He peered at her with conflicting emotion. "So what do we do next?"

"I'll call everyone, remind them of the secrecy surrounding your case."

"Including Sally Ann?" he pressed. Although he had talked to her, he felt Cynthia should, too. He knew how tireless the media could be, and didn't want them wearing her down. Fortunately, her knowing the court was watching her every move in regard to Ryan would go a long way toward insuring her continued silence.

Cynthia nodded. "She's first on the list."

Not seeing anything else that could be done, he turned to go. "Tom—" her soft voice stopped him. She crossed the room to his side and gently touched his arm. "It's going to be all right. I promise you whatever happens next, we'll handle it."

His frustration with her softened somewhat. "Just remember, Cynthia, sometimes you've got to fight. You can't always sit on a fence and let others determine the outcome."

She looked hurt by that, and feeling contrite, realizing none of this was her doing, he leaned over and kissed her cheek, lingering longer than he had a right to. Then he turned and walked out.

As usual during the weekend, lines at the checkout at the grocery store were long. Cynthia amused herself by perusing some of the magazines on display. Her face changed, though, as she saw the cover of the latest *Personalities*. Tom's face was staring back at her.

He was smiling, relaxed—it was obviously a publicity photo used for one of his books. Superimposed on top of that, was a picture of Sally Ann Anderson still in her nursing uniform, her eyes red from crying, tears running down her cheeks.

"Oh, no," Cynthia breathed, already reaching for the magazine so she could get a better look at the damage inflicted on them by Sam Reeb.

She flipped through the magazine hurriedly till she found the story, then began to read. Apparently, Sam Reeb had found out everything, she thought, dismayed, including the fact that Ryan was born via surrogate for a ten-thousand-dollar fee plus expenses.

Cynthia put the magazine down. She had to see Tom. She had to tell him, before he found out elsewhere, or heaven forbid, ran into a display of the magazine himself.

She hurried through the checkout line, going so far as to sack some of the groceries herself, then dashed home to put them away. Sprinting back out to the car, she drove straight to Tom's place.

Jasmine answered the door, a grim look on her face. She had Ryan on her hip. "Tom's not here." Her brusque statement was accompanied by an accusing look.

"Does he—"

"He saw a copy of *Personalities* this morning when he went to the market. He's absolutely livid, and I don't know what he'll do."

Jasmine sighed, then finally decided to trust Cynthia. "He's down the street at the tennis courts, working out." By then, Cynthia was already halfway down the walk. "I don't know if I'd go down there if I were you," Jasmine called after her. "He was boiling."

Precisely why she had to see him, now, Cynthia thought, before Tom did or said anything foolish.

She found him slamming tennis balls against a concrete backdrop between the courts, sweat pouring down his face.

"I take it you've seen it," he said through gritted teeth. His eyes were full of menace, directed, she knew, at Sally Ann, and the no-win situation they all suddenly found themselves in.

"Yes, I saw it." Her chest hurt when she thought of how traumatic it must have been for him, seeing his picture on the cover of a magazine, reading the unfairly slanted story inside.

He swore and slammed the tennis ball against the wall. "She knew she wasn't supposed to talk to the press." Another ball landed against the wall with a loud smack. "She knew that and she still talked to that sleazy Sam Reeb!"

"Tom, please..." Her throat was tight and dry. All she could manage was a whisper. She knew that there was nothing that she or anyone else could say to appease him at that moment.

He stopped hitting the ball and turned to face Cynthia, his breathing ragged. "You want to help? Okay, I'll tell you what you can do. You can tell Ms. Sally Ann Anderson that she had better stay away from me because there is just no telling what I would do to her if I were to see her now." He was shaking he was so angry.

Suddenly she found herself trembling, too, and desperate to comfort him, yet no matter how much she wanted to just wrap her arms around him and ease the anger and bitterness welling up inside him, she dared not. At that moment, she would've liked nothing more than to be able to quit the case, but she was afraid what would happen if she did. Afraid that this untenable situation would be made even worse. And if there was anything she couldn't stand, it was to see Tom or Ryan suffer even more.

"Tom, this will die down," Cynthia soothed.

Tom gave a hoarse, disbelieving laugh. "Like it did for Baby M?" he said. "They're still snapping photos of her, years after the trial." He shook his head derisively. "No, this is just the beginning."

Cynthia was afraid he was right. In the meantime he still had her staunchly on Ryan's side, and in a roundabout way, his. That had to count for something, she thought, didn't it?

SALLY ANN HUDDLED in a cheap motel-room chair, the bedspread wrapped around her thin shoulders. The curtains were drawn against the morning sunlight, and the room was cloaked in a gloom as deep and depressing as her mood.

She had about died that morning when her friend from the hospital gift shop had come by the nurses' station to show her a copy of the latest *Personalities*. It didn't take a genius to realize she had made the biggest mistake of her life in talking to that pushy Sam Reeb. But at the time, he had seemed so sympathetic, so kind, so willing to listen to her side of the story, and before she knew it, all her deepest feelings and thoughts were tumbling out of her mouth.

Then he'd suggested a picture for the cover, to let the public know how upset she was. She'd foolishly agreed.

Now Tom had even more reason to hate her. She'd broken the court order for secrecy, and they might put her in jail for it—if they could find her, that was, which was why she was hiding out in this cheap motel.

She let out a long, anguished sigh. Oh God, what was she going to do? How was she going to get herself out of this mess? And Tom would be even more furious if he knew that she had agreed to accept fifteen thousand dollars from *Personalities*, in payment for a seven-week exclusive on her story.

She hadn't known that at the beginning. It had been after the interview that Sam Reeb had told her it was magazine policy to pay someone for an exclusive story.

Her first inclination had been to tell him she didn't want the money. But when she thought about the lawyer bills, court costs and the fact she needed another car, she accepted the money.

It had arrived the day after she had talked to Sam Reeb and signed the paper guaranteeing *Personalities* exclusive rights. It was in her bank account right now. She hadn't yet had time to go out and buy a car. But she would have to—for when she had custodial rights to Ryan.

But not today.

Today she was just going to stay holed up. She needed rest to figure out how to explain herself to Judge Mitchum and to Cynthia. They were all probably angry at her. But there was no help for it, she

thought defiantly. Her love for her son was too powerful, and it, like everything else, would just have to be
dealt with.

Some way, somewhere, she would find the strength.

Chapter Eight

They had decided that Sally Ann could no longer go to Tom's for her thrice-weekly visitations. Cynthia had offered her house as a neutral meeting place, where both parents could come and go. Wanting to see Ryan's mother as little as possible, Tom had readily agreed.

He felt like he was walking a tightrope. Trying to give Ryan the contact with his mother that he needed and maybe even deserved, while at the same time protecting him from her impulsive, careless side. Trying to get his work done without neglecting his son. Trying to deal with Cynthia without letting his attraction to her, the desire he felt for her, get in the way.

Now Cynthia was at his door, ready to take Ryan to her place. But Tom was hesitant. "I . . . think we need to change our plans a bit, Cynthia. Since he's never been there before, I want to make a trial run, just to make sure he's comfortable there, before we bring Sally Ann into the scene."

There was a silence. Then Cynthia said, "You didn't say anything about this before."

"I didn't really think about it before. Now I think all this is going to confuse him and we need to be extra careful not to upset him in any way."

Frowning, she ran a hand through her hair. "I wish you'd called me earlier." She glanced at her watch. "Sally Ann's supposed to meet me there in thirty minutes."

"Can't you call her, ask her to put off her visit until tomorrow while we make a trial run with Ryan to your place now?"

Cynthia surveyed him steadily for a moment. "I'll try to catch her," she said finally.

She returned a couple of minutes later. "She agreed to your suggestion, but she's not too happy about it."

Aware Cynthia was weighing his every word, he said only, "I'll get Ryan's diaper bag."

By mutual agreement, they took her car, so Ryan could get used to riding in the sporty green BMW. Tom liked the way she handled the small car, her touch sure and easy as it moved from the wheel to the gearshift and back again.

Once at Cynthia's place, to Tom's mixed feelings of relief and surprise, Ryan was not only comfortable but anxious to explore. Holding Cynthia's hand, he toddled right back to the small temporary playroom she'd set up, with its safety gate across the threshold.

Cynthia, whom Tom thought looked particularly fetching in hip-hugging slacks, sat on the floor with Ryan. At her suggestion, Tom left several times and came back, but Ryan was so busy exploring all the new toys in the room that he barely noticed.

There were blocks and balls, stuffed animals, a set of dishes and a miniature kitchen, as well as several riding toys—all of them brand spanking new. "Did you buy all this?" he asked Cynthia, amazed.

She shook her head, and after a moment, reluctantly imparted, "No, Sally Ann did. She brought them over last night."

There were easily two-hundred-dollars worth of toys here, Tom thought. Where did Sally Ann get the money? He'd been under the impression she was living on a tight budget, especially after selling her car to pay back the surrogacy fee. If she was this irresponsible about money, surely she'd be irresponsible about Ryan, too.

He would definitely have to tell his lawyer about this.

Tom dragged his gaze back to Cynthia, watching as Ryan toddled up to impulsively hug her, a hug she returned warmly. She was so good with kids, so gentle. He wondered if she would be as physical and giving in...other relationships. He wondered if her breasts were as soft and high as they looked beneath the silk blouse, her stomach as flat and firm, her hips as lush and round.

He had to stop this daydreaming about her. She wasn't a character in one of his books, or even a potential model for one....

"How is your work going?" Cynthia asked abruptly.

"Not well, actually," Tom admitted.

It didn't help that Toby called him almost daily to check up on him. Toby was worried about the effects the custody case, which thanks to *Personalities* he now knew about, was having on him.

Ryan had plopped down beside Cynthia and sunk his teeth into a pretzel-shaped blue teething ring. Now he rested his head against her. Watching, it was all Tom could do not to groan with envy.

"Do you have writer's block?" Cynthia asked.

"I don't believe in writer's block. It's true there are days when the words don't come easily, but that's usually because I haven't thought through the plot action enough. Proper outlining and a fairly relaxed writing schedule usually take care of it."

"Oh." She looked intrigued. Ryan hopped off her lap, but her blouse remained slightly rumpled, molding to her breasts. Tom found the sight disconcerting. She shifted position, crossing her legs, and said, "If you don't have writer's block, what's the problem then?"

He laughed humorlessly. "It's hard to write with a glib, devil-may-care tone when my mood is the exact opposite."

"So your work is sounding as wretched as you feel?"

Her soft, sympathetic tone acted like a balm on his ravaged nerves. Tom shrugged, and one leg pulled up to his chest, rested his chin on his bent knee, dimly aware that Ryan wasn't the only one who felt cozy and at home. "Toby, my editor, certainly thinks so."

"What are you going to do?" she asked gently, and for a moment he wanted to drown in the softness of her hazel eyes.

"I don't know. I'll tell you what I'm not going to do, though. I'm not going to go out and paint the town red like he wants me to do."

NOW THAT THE DOOR IS OPEN...
Peel off the bouquet and send it on the postpaid order card to receive:

4 FREE BOOKS
from

An attractive 20k gold electroplated chain FREE! And a mystery gift as an EXTRA BONUS!

PLUS

FREE HOME DELIVERY!
Once you receive your 4 FREE books and gifts, you'll be able to open your door to more great romance reading month after month. Enjoy the convenience of previewing 4 brand-new books every month delivered right to your home months before they appear in stores. Each book is yours for the low members only price of $2.74* — that's 21 cents off the retail cover price — with no additional charges for home delivery.

SPECIAL EXTRAS — FREE!
You'll also receive the "Heart to Heart" Newsletter FREE with every book shipment. Every issue is filled with interviews, news about upcoming books and more! And as a valued reader, we'll be sending you additional free gifts from time to time — as a token of our appreciation.

NO-RISK GUARANTEE!
- There's no obligation to buy — and the free books and gifts are yours to keep forever.
- You pay the low members' only price and receive books months before they appear in stores.
- You may cancel at any time, for any reason, just by sending us a note or a shipping statement marked "cancel" or by returning any shipment of books to us at our cost. Either way the free books and gifts are yours to keep!

RETURN THE POSTPAID ORDER CARD TODAY AND OPEN YOUR DOOR TO THESE 4 EXCITING LOVE-FILLED NOVELS. THEY ARE YOURS ABSOLUTELY FREE ALONG WITH YOUR 20k GOLD ELECTROPLATED CHAIN AND MYSTERY GIFT.

*Terms and prices subject to change without notice.
 Sales tax applicable in NY and Iowa.
© 1989 Harlequin Enterprises Ltd.

FREE! 20k GOLD ELECTROPLATED CHAIN!

You'll love this 20k gold electroplated chain! The necklace is finely crafted with 160 double-soldered links and is electroplate finished in genuine 20k gold. It's nearly ⅛" wide, fully 20" long — and has the look and feel of the real thing. "Glamorous" is the perfect word for it, and it is yours free with this offer!

HARLEQUIN READER SERVICE
901 FUHRMANN BLVD
PO BOX 1867
BUFFALO NY 14240-9952

Place the
Bouquet
here →

Yes! I have attached the bouquet above. Please rush me my four Harlequin AMERICAN ROMANCE® novels along with my FREE 20k Electroplated Gold Chain and mystery gift as explained on the opposite page. I understand that accepting these books and gifts places me under no obligation ever to buy any books. I may cancel at any time for any reason, and the free books and gifts will be mine to keep!   154 CIH NBJC
(U-H-A-03/90)

Name _____

Address _____ Apt. _____

City _____ State _____

Zip _____

Offer limited to one per household and not valid for present Harlequin American Romance subscribers. Terms and prices subject to change without notice. Orders subject to approval.

PRINTED IN U.S.A.

© 1989 Harlequin Enterprises Ltd.

PLACE THE BOUQUET ON THIS CARD. FILL IT OUT AND MAIL TODAY!

Take this beautiful
20k GOLD
ELECTROPLATED CHAIN
with your 4 FREE BOOKS
PLUS A MYSTERY GIFT
If offer card is missing, write to: Harlequin Reader Service,
901 Fuhrmann Blvd., P.O. Box 1867, Buffalo, NY 14269-1867.

PLACE THE BOUQUET ON THIS CARD. FILL IT OUT AND MAIL TODAY!

Cynthia's bow-shaped mouth thinned disparagingly. "He doesn't realize that, um, catting around would be bad for your case?" Cynthia said.

"He thinks I can be discreet," Tom said dryly.

Cynthia's mouth crooked up in a knowing smile, giving Tom the distinct impression she'd done her own share of partying in the past. "But . . . you don't want to," Cynthia said slowly.

For a second, Tom held her gaze. Her amusement faded, to be replaced by something he couldn't quite identify, something she looked vaguely afraid of. Was it possible she was feeling the same sexual vibes?

The moment passed, and they talked some more, about trivial matters, but the tension still hung in the air. Then Tom glanced at his watch, relieved to see the visit was over. It was getting almost too close in there again, he thought, too intimate.

Cynthia stood, too, also looking less burdened.

They were almost to the door when the bell rang.

No sooner had Cynthia opened the door, than Sally Ann stepped in eagerly. "Hi, I just wanted to see how it went with—" Seeing Tom and Ryan still there, she stopped in midsentence. Her face drained of color, then turned bright red.

Ryan, oblivious, toddled over to her and said, "Mama!" as he grabbed her around the knees.

The word was like a knife to Tom's heart. It made the threat of losing Ryan all the more real. Confused, hurting, he remained where he stood with effort, aware of a fierce burning in his throat.

Sally Ann extricated Ryan's arms from her knees, and still holding gently to his hands, she knelt to hug him. And once again the emotion Tom saw flowing there was a lethal blow to his heart. Because for the first time he became aware there might come a time in the future when Ryan wanted to be with his mother every bit as much or more than he wanted to be with him.

"Hi, sweetie," she said softly, lovingly.

"Mama!" Ryan cried.

The unbridled happiness in Ryan's voice was suddenly too much for Tom. Knowing only that he had to get out of there, he pivoted and started for the back porch he'd glimpsed off Cynthia's kitchen. As he pushed outside, he could feel himself falling apart inside. Not wanting anyone to see him dissolve into tears, which to his horror was a distinct possibility, he continued on until he was standing in the small, heavily treed backyard. He took a deep breath. And then another, and another. Nonetheless, it was long minutes later before he knew with any real certainty that he was going to be okay, that he could be a calm, controlled human being for Ryan.

It seemed an eternity before he heard a car start up and take off. The back door slammed and Cynthia, carrying Ryan, walked out to his side. Seeing his father, Ryan held out his arms. "Da! Da!"

Tom took him gratefully into his arms, and his weight and warmth had never felt so good, so reassuring.

Her eyes wide and searching as she looked at him, Cynthia said gently, "Sally Ann didn't realize I had driven you and Ryan over here. She thought you'd be long gone by now, and when she drove by she didn't see your Bronco out front. She just wanted to know how it went, if she would be able to see Ryan tomorrow as scheduled.'' The excuses were valid, but he felt himself growing grimmer nonetheless. Sensing his anger, Cynthia frowned. "Have a heart, Tom," she said sharply. "You're not the only parent involved here. She loves him and wants to spend time with him, too."

Tom knew that was true; Ryan was a hard child not to love. But as for Sally Ann being a real parent to him, he still had his doubts. For a while he didn't say anything; neither did Cynthia. Knowing the stalemate had to end sometime, he sighed and said, "What did you tell her about tomorrow night?" Reluctance tinged his every word.

There was no mercy in Cynthia's voice, or her quelling look. "That she's on for it, and the night after that—to make up for the visitation she missed tonight." She hesitated, and started again, her voice softer now, more compelling, "We have to go forward, Tom. Ryan was okay here tonight, and as you just saw he is growing very fond of his mother."

Tom knew that. Unfortunately, his emotions were still in such turmoil he didn't trust himself to speak, for fear of what he might say. Aware he was being rude, he muttered tersely, "It's late. Ryan and I have to get home."

She stared at him in silence, looking for a moment as if she wanted to bridge the difference, soothe him somehow. But the moment passed. Dropping her gaze, she said, "I'll get my keys."

They didn't speak on the drive home. There seemed nothing to say.

To Cynthia's satisfaction, Ryan's first two visits to her home without his father went smoothly. He played and cuddled with Sally Ann, and never evidenced any anxiety.

Ryan's father, however, was another story, Cynthia reflected. With only a week and a half left before the April-twelfth hearing, Tom had retreated into his work. Oh, he still cooperated with her, but it was as if there was a wall between them now. She felt she was seeing only what he wanted her to see, and it disturbed her to be held so deliberately at arm's length. Lately, Tom had made her feel like the enemy, along with Sally Ann. And it was a feeling she didn't like. She'd tried so hard to remain impartial, fair.

She knew he must feel threatened by Ryan's growing closeness to Sally Ann. She sympathized with him, but she also knew babies needed their mothers.

Determined to talk to him about his attitude, and maybe about how his writing was going, she stayed after dropping Ryan off after Sally Ann's visitation.

Tom's frown deepened as he returned to the living room after putting Ryan to bed, and saw the notebook, and the intrusion into his life that it represented, but he didn't walk away. She let out her breath slowly.

Suddenly, out on the street in front of Tom's house, a car honked, long and obnoxiously. Simultaneously, the doorbell rang. Frowning, Tom excused himself to get the door.

The laughter was the first to float back to her. Feminine, sultry voices, and then a man, urging jovially, "Come on, pal. I've got the ladies and the champagne chilling out in the limo, just like I promised. If this doesn't get you in a 007 mood, I don't know what will!'' Cynthia heard more laughter, and then a feminine voice purred, ''It'll be therapeutic for you get out and dance until dawn, Tommy. You know how much we all love to dance.''

A chill went down Cynthia's spine as she heard the unmistakably sensual promise in the voice. Telling herself it was really none of her business, she picked up her briefcase. Beyond, Tom was trying hard to get rid of the unexpected revelers. ''Look, please go, all of you,'' she heard him hissing as she rounded the corner and entered the front hall.

''Oh!'' The blond man in the tux did a double take when he saw Cynthia and let out a low whistle.

Cynthia blushed, and Tom groaned and put a hand to his face. The blond man grinned even wider as his glance traveled the length of her body and then back up again.

For a moment Cynthia was so flustered by his outrageously predatory behavior that she couldn't place him. And then she finally remembered who he was— Toby Williams, Tom's editor. But, judging by the wolfish expression on Toby's face, he didn't remember who she was. Which gave her the advantage, Cynthia thought.

Toby flashed Cynthia another lady-killing grin and jumped to his own conclusions. ''Oh, now I get it....'' He gave Tom an aggrieved look. ''Now I know why you were so hot to get rid of us—you've already got yourself company for the evening! Well, hey, she can come along,'' he continued enthusiastically. Holding up a magnum of champagne, he said, "The more the merrier, I always say. What do you say, good-lookin'? Want to go out and party hearty?"

It looked to Cynthia like Toby had already been partying heartily. Maybe all the way from New York. Was this what Tom's past had been like, the reason he had never married? she wondered, dismayed. Was this the kind of jaunt Tom had not wanted Toby to mention the previous time they'd met? And what effect would such carousing have on Ryan?

"Don't mind me," Cynthia said, edging past, "I'm just leaving."

Tom's hand shot out to touch her arm. "Stay," he said meaningfully, his eyes boring into hers, "and let me introduce you to Toby's friends." Glancing at the two women, he looked at a loss for their names.

"Wanda and Libby," Toby drawled.

"How do you do." Gathering her composure, Cynthia nodded at both. They nodded back.

"And this, Toby," Tom said in a voice that was heavy with warning, "is Cynthia Whittiker, attorney. She's in charge of Ryan's custody, remember?"

"Sure, I remember her. She—" Suddenly, all the color drained from his face. "Oh, no," he said under his breath.

Oh, no was right, Cynthia thought. Toby couldn't have put it any better.

"She's the attorney who's been determining my fitness as a parent," Tom continued dryly, more amused now than annoyed.

Toby said to the two scantily clad women beside him, "Maybe you two better wait in the limo." Toby turned back to Cynthia and Tom, his expression sheepish. "I, uh, guess I should have called first, huh? It's just I was determined to get Tom out of this blue funk he's been in and back to writing about dashing deeds, and I thought if any two women could do it, Wanda and Libby could—"

"Maybe you better stop while you're ahead," Tom interjected on a pained sigh.

Cynthia was almost beginning to enjoy the discomfiture of the two men. It was almost as if she'd caught them with their hands in the cookie jar. Certainly, this was a more telling insight to Tom's past, and perhaps his current character, than anything else she had learned lately.

Tom looked at her. He didn't seem to like the fact she was beginning to enjoy herself. Toby, deciding he'd had enough, made his excuses and trotted back to the limo waiting at the curb. He'd barely stepped inside before it took off at a roar.

Cynthia grinned. And to think had she not stuck around to talk to Tom, she would have missed it.

Tom shut the door. "I didn't know he was coming."

She grinned again, wider this time. "Obviously."

He swallowed, a bit put off by her amusement. She wondered if she hadn't been there, if Jasmine could have baby-sat for him, would Tom have gone out with Toby, for old time's sake? And how would she have felt about it if he had? The revelation she wouldn't have liked it was unsettling. Surely she couldn't be jealous, could she?

Her smile faded into a frown.

Misinterpreting the reason behind the frown, Tom said, "It's true, in my single days I did go out with Toby... and various girls whose names I can't remember. But it was only out of a sense of duty."

Cynthia found that a little hard to believe. She gave him a droll look. He persisted, "Come on, give me a break. Those two starlets definitely are not, never were, my type."

Looking at the sincere expression on his face, she could almost believe him. But maybe that was because she wanted to believe him. Was it for Ryan's sake? Or for her own?

"I'm a fit parent," he continued.

And a very sexy man, too, she couldn't help but note for the hundredth time. A man with no apparent involvement. Somehow, she managed to find her voice. "I don't remember saying you weren't a fit parent."

"Maybe not, but you were thinking it—at least for a few seconds there."

She *had* been annoyed with him. Very. And for reasons that were so complex she didn't want to think about them. She should just reassure him and leave. Still, she hadn't done what she'd originally intended— that is, ask him about his hostile attitude. That, however, seemed unimportant now—clearly he was no longer hostile—but this was her chance to learn more about him, to get him to open up to her. With her recommendation as per Ryan's custody due in ten days, could she afford to pass it up? She thought not. "All right, I admit," she said finally, not quite meeting his searching gaze, "that this episode has opened up a few questions in my mind."

One hand touching her shoulder, he guided her into the living room. "Such as?" he prompted, taking a wing chair.

She sat down on the sofa facing him, and suddenly aware of the way her above-the-knee skirt tended to creep up when she sat down, demurely crossed her ankles. "In all the time I've been interviewing and observing you, we haven't really talked about the possibility of your getting married in the future if you were to meet someone special."

No sooner had she voiced the question than Tom was up and roaming the room. "I find the question irrelevant. And questions about my past, intrusive. If you were in my position, I don't think you'd answer them."

"If the tables were turned, I certainly would."

"Ha!" he scoffed, stepping nearer. His arms dropped to his sides. His dark hair shimmered in the softly lighted room. "That's easy for you to say. Not so easy to do."

Amused now, she said boldly, "I disagree."

"Fine," he said, sauntering closer. "Then let's put it to the test and just see how comfortable you are discussing the intimate details of your private life, how willing you are to delve deep into your feelings." He sat opposite her again. "Have you ever been married?"

Her hand on the arm of the sofa, she started to get up. He placed his hand over hers to stop her. Suddenly she was aware of many things. That his hand was very warm and sure over hers. That his palm was slightly callused. That the muscled look of his thighs was no lie. That there was a fluttering deep inside her, a willingness to be kissed, right alongside the certainty that it would not happen, no matter how much she might wish it so.

She was also aware that he was right—she didn't like this third degree from him any more than he liked it from her. And also, that he was just as curious about her—on a personal level—as she was about him.

Ever so slowly, he released his light but tantalizing grip on her hand. She stared at him, wide-eyed, her pulse racing. She struggled to regain her professionalism.

Deciding his question was fair, she said, "A few years ago, yes, I was married."

"What happened?" he asked softly, and something in her began to melt.

I can't do this, she thought, *I can't let him get close to me.* But mesmerized by the genuine interest in his dark blue eyes she heard herself answer, "We had fundamental differences . . . so we divorced."

"What kind of fundamental differences?" he asked.

She floundered. "There . . . were a lot of things."

"Tell me," he said, with such unexpected gentleness she caught her breath.

And she saw then he really did want to know. "We married while we were still in law school."

"You were both students?" His voice was even softer now, gently caressing her ravaged nerves.

"Yes." Her eyes closed as she went back to that awful time in her life. She had never really talked about it much, largely because it was so painful, but she had the feeling that if anyone could understand what she'd been through, Tom could. "We each had a little less than a half year to go and my husband and I wanted to start a family. We figured I could have the baby while waiting to pass the bar exam, and then go to work— probably on a part-time basis, after that. Unfortunately it didn't work out as we had planned. When I didn't get pregnant within six months, he wanted us to go for fertility tests." Cynthia remembered how that had scared her. She'd gone to the doctor reluctantly, only to be told there really was no problem her own body wouldn't remedy, given time. "My gynecologist told me I wasn't ovulating, and that it was probably only a temporary condition—maybe due to stress. He recommended we give it another six months. See if my system would straighten out on its own. The only option was for them to put me on fertility pills."

"But you didn't want to get into all that?" he guessed.

She answered sadly, "I wanted a baby, too, but I also knew we had plenty of time for it to happen. I figured it would when the time was right. I was also under a great deal of pressure, trying to finish up and prepare for the bar exam. I thought the doctor was right, that it was simply stress keeping us from conceiving. I felt things would work out given time. But . . ."

"But your husband didn't agree with you?"

"No." Her fatalistic approach put him off, Cynthia admitted, and after several years together, they finally went their separate ways. She'd been hurt, deeply so. But at least she didn't have to live with the idea she had let someone close to her down in a fundamental, heartbreaking way.

Tom was quiet, absorbing all she had told him. "I'm sorry," he said simply. "I know what it is to want a child and not be able to have one." When he met her gaze again, he looked oddly vulnerable. "I, too, kept thinking that if I were just patient enough everything would work out all right, I would find the perfect woman."

He shook his head, as if realizing now what a fruitless dream that had been, what a waste of time. "But when I headed toward my forties I knew I'd waited almost too long, that I hadn't done nearly enough to make it happen, and that if I didn't take a more active role in securing my own fate I'd lose out." He leaned toward her earnestly. "I wanted a child while I was still young and energetic enough to be a good father. If what I did makes me an anomaly in everyone else's eyes, so be it." He wasn't changing.

"Do you have any regrets?" she asked softly.

He shook his head. "Ryan's the best thing that's ever happened to me."

She was suddenly aware they'd been talking too long, and far too familiarly, that they were very close to achieving the sort of intimacy they mustn't share. Not until the court case was decided. Maybe not afterward. She got up abruptly, knowing she had to leave while she still had the will. "I'd better go."

Disappointment flickered in his eyes. "I'll walk you out."

He stopped her at the car. "Cynthia, about what happened tonight with Toby... You understand he just came down here to cheer me up, that in his way he felt he was doing me a favor."

She paused, not sure it was that simple. "I'm concerned about his influence on Ryan."

"Ryan's just a baby!"

"But he won't always be, and Ryan will model his own behavior on that of the adults around him, especially the male adults."

Silence. The starlight revealed his face in stark angles and planes, and she could see the sudden tension in the set of his mouth. "Is what happened tonight going in your report?" Now they were down to brass tacks.

She would have liked to say no, but she couldn't in good conscience omit anything she observed about Tom or Sally Ann. She moved back a pace, holding her briefcase in front of her knees with both hands. She didn't want to upset Tom after the closeness they had shared, but she had to tell him the truth. "I have no choice," she said finally. His face tightened even more and she hurried to reassure him, "I'll do my best to put it in perspective for the judge."

Again he was silent, his blue eyes both hurt and stormy. He seemed to sense there was no use in arguing the point with her, but he didn't try to hide his disappointment. It was obvious he would have preferred she not mention Toby's performance that night at all.

He sighed heavily. "I understand," he said tersely, turning back toward the house. "Do what you have to."

She would, Cynthia thought, as she watched him go. She only wished her job wasn't so difficult to do, that she didn't sometimes feel so connected to him. If only she had met Tom and gotten to know him some other way, how much easier and more fulfilling their lives could have been...

Chapter Nine

"I don't understand why you're being so stubborn," Tom Sr. said, when he called long distance early the next morning. "Just talk to this reporter friend of mine and tell him your side of the story."

"I can't do that, Dad." Tom passed a hand wearily over his eyes. What a way to start the day, he thought. He hadn't even gotten out of bed yet and already his father was on his case.

"Then let me talk to him for you," Tom Sr. countered persuasively.

"No!" Tom couldn't stop the vehement note in his voice. He knew the press was bugging everyone close to him; literally everyone in his family had called him in the past week to let him know they'd been approached about interviews, and/or offered money for private family pictures of Ryan and Tom. All had refused, of course, which only made the reporters more tenacious and insistent.

His father sighed loudly, but when he spoke again his voice was gentle. "Listen to me, son. Ryan already is in the news whether you like it or not. So you have a choice. You can let the reporters write the story on hearsay, or you can let them write it truthfully. Now, I have a friend who's been through a custody battle himself and he's very sympathetic to your cause. He could write a story that would help people to understand how much Ryan means to you, what you've been through the past few months. He could help people understand that a father is every bit as important to a child as the mother, if not more so, as in your case. With the trial only a week away, it's important we get public sympathy on your side."

"Dad, this isn't a jury trial," Tom explained, his patience strained to the absolute limit. "Judge Mitchum is going to decide which of us gets custody."

"He can still be influenced by public opinion, as can Cynthia Whittiker. And right now public sympathy is on Sally Ann's side! She even has feminist groups picketing on her behalf in front of the courthouse."

Tom knew—he'd seen it on the news the day before. Sally Ann had not solicited their support, hadn't even been to any of the demonstrations, but still, they were having an impact, keeping Ryan's upcoming custody trial in the news almost daily.

He couldn't let himself worry about that. "Dad, I've met Judge Mitchum. I really think he's going to try to be fair. And as for Cynthia, I know she'll do what she thinks is right for Ryan, regardless of popular opinion." He admired that part of her character as much as he feared it, because right now, as things stood today, he sensed she still had a great deal of sympathy for Sally Ann's plight. Maybe because they were both women, maybe because Sally Ann loved Ryan and vice versa. As painful as it was for him to admit that, he knew it was true. He just didn't know if Sally Ann's love would benefit Ryan in the long run, or hurt him. And heaven knew he would do anything and everything in his power to keep Ryan from being hurt.

"You're making a mistake," Tom Sr. warned.

"It's mine to make, Dad."

A long silence ensued. "If you change your mind about the press—"

"I won't," Tom said.

His father paused. "You aren't the only one who stands to be hurt here," he said thickly. "We love Ryan, too."

And, Tom thought, his parents didn't feel Tom was doing enough for Ryan.

The silent disapproval hurt.

Unfortunately, Tom's day didn't get any better. Toby called, with a list of revisions he needed on the series outlines. Tom promised to get to them right away, but it meant he would be up half the night working and would probably have to work most of the weekend, as well. Then, when Tom took Ryan to his pediatrician for his checkup that afternoon, Ryan had to have a shot.

And then he had a reaction.

"Rough way to end the day, huh, buddy?" Tom murmured sympathetically the following evening, as he slid his squalling son into tepid bath water. Although Ryan normally liked baths, he didn't appreciate having to take one when he had a fever; but it was the quickest way to bring his temperature down, get him comfortable again. It also prevented febrile convulsions.

Tom couldn't blame him for feeling grumpy. He was always grumpy when he got sick, too. Talking soothingly to his son all the while, Tom held out his hands. Verbally nixing the idea of a drink, Ryan let him pick him up, and his head rested on Tom's shoulder as he walked out to the kitchen.

Tom had just poured a cup of Ryan's favorite apple-grape juice when the doorbell rang. With Ryan still in his arms, he went to get it. To his mixed feelings of surprise and pleasure, Cynthia was standing on the steps. "I came as soon as I heard," she said. "Is Ryan all right?".

Tom nodded, touched that she cared so much about his son—and not just in an official capacity, but in a way that seemed to come straight from her heart. He had only called her because he felt that she, as Ryan's guardian, ought to be aware of the situation. With the court case coming up, he wasn't taking any chances on being accused of acting irresponsibly. "It's just a reaction from the vaccination he had yesterday. He'll be all right in another twenty-four hours. The main thing is to keep him comfortable and hydrated."

She peered at Tom consideringly, the sympathy she felt for him clearly evident on her face. "You look exhausted."

Tom shut the door and, remembering Ryan's need of fluids, led the way back to his kitchen. "I am. I was up until midnight working on some outlines, and then—" he couldn't quite stifle a yawn "—Ryan got up at three this morning. He hasn't been asleep since. He won't let me put him down."

"You don't have any help?" Cynthia asked, looking around.

She probably expected Jasmine to be there, he thought. And under normal circumstances, she might have been. "Frank's home from Alaska for a long weekend. I didn't want to disturb the family, since they're all together so infrequently."

"You could've called your parents."

He didn't answer. His dad lecturing him on the need to go to the press again? No way.

Her gaze rested on Ryan's fever-flushed cheeks, before returning to Tom's face. "You look like you could use some help tonight." Her voice was soft and matter of fact. "Do you want me to stay?"

A wave of gratitude swept through him. He never would have asked her, but he was glad she had offered. "Do you mind?" He found he was holding his breath as he waited for her answer.

"No, I had nothing else planned tonight."

For reasons that seemed silly and juvenile even as they occurred to him, he was glad she didn't have a date. What that might mean, in turn, he didn't want to think about. He wasn't getting a crush on Cynthia Whittiker because... well, he just wouldn't let that happen. She was judging him enough as it was, always watching everything he did and said and thought.

Maybe it would be too awkward, difficult, having her here with him this evening.

Then again, what choice did he have? He was truly exhausted, and he really needed someone to spell him. Someone who had a soothing affect on Ryan—and him. And that discounted Sally Ann right there, because just seeing her still made him tense. He didn't want to think about what it would be like dealing with her in court the next week.

Abruptly, he became aware Cynthia was now staring at him in the same curious, bemused way he had just been staring at her. Her attention, discreet and subdued as it was, was so unsettling he found he had to turn away.

"Uh, thanks for offering to help me out," he said, picking up the cup of juice. "I appreciate it."

His attention completely on his son, he brought the cup of juice up to Ryan's mouth. Ryan accepted it only momentarily, before pushing it away with both hands. Unfortunately he didn't have the grasp he thought he did on the cup, and before he knew it, it was slipping from his hands. Cynthia saw what was happening and managed to catch the cup before it hit the floor; nonetheless sticky dark red juice splashed up, covering the white knit sweater she wore.

Looking at the mess, Tom swore. Why couldn't it have been his clothes that were stained? "I'm sorry." He looked at her, expecting the worst.

"That's okay, really."

He was relieved to see she was smiling as she moved to the sink, and dabbed ineffectually at the stain splattered like purplish raindrops across her front.

"That's part grape juice," Tom said worriedly, hoping the stain would come out. But he knew, from months of doing Ryan's laundry, the chances were slim, unless proper action was taken right away. "I think you better take that off and soak it in cold water," Tom said, already heading for his bedroom.

Cynthia frowned but relented. "You're probably right."

Tom was already heading back to his bedroom. "I'll get you a shirt of mine to wear."

He returned seconds later with an ironed blue oxford-cloth shirt. "I think this'll do." He thrust the shirt at her, still feeling a little embarrassed and ill at ease about what had just happened. If he hadn't been so tired, he told himself, he would have caught that cup before it fell, or at least anticipated what Ryan had been about to do. But the truth was he had been so busy looking at Cynthia and thinking about her he'd been aware of little else.

Blushing slightly, she accepted the shirt with thanks, then disappeared into the guest bathroom off the laundry room. Seconds later, she came out, looking better in the shirt than he ever had. "Any luck getting the stain out?" Tom asked, looking over at her hopefully.

"I think it's starting to soak out a little, but it'll be a while before we'll know for sure." She noticed the can in his hand. Glancing down at Ryan, who was now completely subdued, she smiled. "What are you two up to?"

"I thought I'd fix him some soup," Tom said.

He figured the activity would help him get his mind off her. And it might have worked, too, if she hadn't looked so darn great in his shirt. There was also something very intimate about the fact she was wearing his clothes. He shrugged off the thought, and the attendant erotic fantasy it spawned. There was his writer's imagination going into overdrive again. He couldn't let that happen.

"Would you mind holding him for a second?" Tom handed Ryan over to her.

She held out her arms, ready to take him; but as Tom half expected, Ryan refused to go. "No," he said adamantly, turning around and clutching Tom's shirt with both fists. The message was clear, Tom thought with an exhausted sigh. Ryan still wanted only him to hold him.

"No problem. I can fix the soup," Cynthia said cheerfully, not the least bit offended by Ryan's uncooperative attitude. To Ryan, she said, "And I don't blame you for only wanting your daddy."

Within a short while, she'd prepared an entire meal. After they'd eaten, Tom's exhaustion finally overtook him and he had to nap awhile. He put Ryan to bed, then after casting her a deeply grateful look, went to lie down.

It wasn't long before Cynthia had the kitchen cleaned up, the dishwasher running. At loose ends, she looked in on Ryan and found he was fast asleep. Tom had left his bedroom door cracked. The absence of sound coming from his room told her he was asleep, too.

She went out to the car and retrieved her briefcase, then got out a paper and pen. Before she'd gotten the news that Ryan was sick, she had been toying over an idea of how to help her mother.

To her dismay, Faith was still holding tight to the idea of a forced early retirement, due to the injured nerves in her right hand. Watching how depressed her mother was becoming, how isolated, Cynthia knew she had to do something. She supposed she was learning from Tom.

She had called the dean of the music school and was told he had offered Faith a part-time job as a lecturer—she was quite an authority on baroque music—but that Faith had turned it down.

Cynthia understood that—sort of. It would be painful for her mother to return to her former workplace less than one hundred percent. But Faith couldn't just do nothing for the rest of her life, Cynthia knew. She had to find a way to go on that was satisfying to her on a creative artistic level. Unfortunately, Faith refused to do that, too, so Cynthia was taking matters into her own hands. She was writing to other music schools in the central Texas area to see if they had room for Faith on their staff in some capacity.

It wasn't the usual way to go about looking for a job, but it was the only way Cynthia could think to help her mother.

She had just finished the fourth letter when she heard Ryan begin to stir. Cynthia went back to the nursery. The little guy was lying in his crib, looking very unhappy. Concerned about the flushed hue of his skin, she put a hand to the back of his cheek. His skin was warm, though not alarmingly so. In fact, he felt slightly cooler than he had earlier.

Deciding to be on the safe side, she wound up the mobile over his bed, located the thermometer and took his temperature. It was ninety-nine point six.

"Well," Cynthia said, checking his diaper and finding it damp. "It's not time for more Tylenol," she said, changing his diaper quickly, with an expertise gained in her years of baby-sitting as a teenager. "But you probably could use a drink. I saw some apple juice in the fridge." She finished the last of the snaps and then lifted Ryan out of the crib. "Want to try that?" she asked.

Ryan nodded, snuggling close. "Drink," he said.

Being as quiet as possible, so as not to wake Tom, Cynthia took Ryan to the kitchen. Holding him on her left hip, Cynthia poured some juice. Ryan downed it thirstily and asked for more, a sure sign he was feeling better.

Finished, they headed back to the living room, where Cynthia grabbed a handful of books. "Want a story, Ryan?" she asked.

He nodded and cuddled close.

Cynthia sat down in the reclinable rocker and situated him on her lap. As they got comfortable, she felt an unexpected maternal warmth for Tom's son. She had a glimpse of what it must be like to be a parent, and for not the first time in her life, she realized what she was missing by not having a child of her own.

Pushing the disturbing thought away, she began to read.

Four stories later, Ryan had fallen back to sleep. Cynthia was getting drowsy, too, but with Ryan snuggled close in her arms, still rocking gently, she was just too comfortable to move. She would put him down in a minute, she thought. In just another minute....

TOM AWOKE WITH A START just after midnight. For a second, he couldn't get his bearings or figure out why he was stretched out, fully-clothed on top of his covers. Then he remembered. Ryan was sick. He glanced at the clock. Almost five hours had passed.

Like a shot, he was up and out of his bed, and going down the hall to Ryan's room. The light was on, the crib empty.

His panicky steps increased as he headed for the living room, but what he saw there made him smile. Ryan was cuddled in Cynthia's arms, his head against the soft fullness of her breast, his mouth slightly open, a baby blanket covering his lower half. The chair was back into the recline position, and Cynthia was sound asleep, too, her arms wrapped protectively around Ryan.

They looked so content, sleeping there, Tom thought with a grin. He had to hand it to Cynthia—she had a soothing affect on both him and his son. But then, he supposed, that wasn't surprising. He'd never met a kinder, more instinctively empathetic woman. Beneath her warm sophistication, there was a very tender side.

Deciding to leave them there, just like that unless one of them awoke, he sank quietly down on the sofa. Moments later, he was asleep again. And as it happened, no one stirred until almost five in the morning.

Cynthia was the first to awake, and within seconds Ryan and Tom had opened their eyes, too. She smiled sleepily, then realized with a start that she'd better leave; the scene was far too domestic for her peace of mind.

Handing Ryan to Tom, she avoided looking too directly at Tom. She stood, stretched, then picked up her briefcase. "I'd better go," she said. "Call me if you need anything else." She whirled and headed for the door.

"I will," Tom said, moving forward to assist her in retrieving her sweater and then show her out, Ryan still in his arms.

The last glimpse he had of her was as she slipped out the door. The sight of her thick chestnut hair, still tousled from sleep, and the damp spot beside her mouth where Ryan had kissed, made his pulse race.

Ryan hadn't been the only one who wanted to kiss her this morning. And thank her. And otherwise transmit an affection too unexpected, and too fragile, to put into words.

But he couldn't do that.

And so he just simply stood and watched as she backed her sporty green BMW out of the drive, and drove away.

"YOU'RE GETTING very emotionally involved with all the participants in the Anderson versus Harrigan custody case, aren't you honey?" Faith said Tuesday afternoon.

Cynthia had dropped by with a few flowers for her mother's garden, and at four o'clock, found her still in her lounging pajamas, watching reruns on television and eating fudge brownies.

Rather than concentrate on her worry over her mother's continued depression and resultant inactivity, Cynthia had launched into a nonstop recitation of her work week, which included tales of Ryan and his father.

"What do you mean?" Cynthia asked, a little embarrassed to think she had revealed so much of her feelings.

Too restless to sit still and endure her mother's searching glance, Cynthia began straightening up the family room. Since her mother's initial spate of housecleaning, upon her arrival home from rehab, she had gone downhill. Old newspapers cluttered the room, and often she didn't even bother to get dressed but rather lounged away the day in her pajamas, robe and slippers.

Faith shook her head, undeterred by her daughter's evasion. "I mean you talk about Tom and Sally Ann and little Ryan as if they were all connected to you somehow, and I don't just mean through the case. I mean as . . . more than that."

Cynthia turned. Was it that obvious, how close she felt to Tom and his little boy? How sympathetic she was to Sally Ann's plight, too? Yes, Sally Ann had made a mistake in giving up her child, but she still loved him very much and more importantly, Ryan loved her, too.

"It's just a very complex problem, Mom, and with my decision due next week, they're all constantly in my thoughts." Tom especially.

Faith made a dissenting sound. Behind her oversize glasses, her eyes clouded with worry. "Be careful, honey. I don't want you hurt when this trial is over."

"You think I will be?" she asked, surprised.

Her mother shrugged. "I just don't know what purpose you would have to see any of them again, once this dispute is decided. And if you've become so close to them, well . . ."

Cynthia refused to think about that.

"UH-OH, IT LOOKS LIKE we've got company again," Cynthia said to Ryan as she pulled into Tom's driveway. Although none of the reporters were allowed on Tom's property, they got as close as they were able. Zoom lenses were adjusted and shutters clicked as she got out of the car, removed Ryan from his seat and rushed him into the house.

Tom was waiting anxiously. "How'd his time with Sally Ann go?" he asked, taking Ryan. "Any trouble with reporters there?"

Cynthia shook her head. "No, but only because they didn't know we'd arranged for today's visitation to take place at the county children's home, instead of my place or Sally Ann's. If they'd gotten wind of the last-minute switch in plans, I'm sure they would've been there in full force."

Ryan squirmed until Tom put him down. He toddled urgently toward the sliding glass doors, then pointed in the direction of his sandbox.

Tom slid open the patio door, helped Ryan down the steps and followed him out into the backyard. It was a warm breezy day, and as Cynthia stepped out beside Tom, she reveled in the feeling of spring all around her.

Without warning, the back gate opened. Jasmine walked in, flanked by her twin boys. "Guess what? I just had an offer from the *National Tattletale*. They'll give me five hundred dollars to tell my version of your story."

"Yeah, more, if we get some pictures," Wes said.

"Did you see all those television trucks parked across the street?" Whit exclaimed.

Tom swore and rolled his eyes. Cynthia knew how he felt.

"I can't even leave the house anymore during the day without them snapping photos," Tom lamented. "I even had a camera crew follow me to the grocery store on Tuesday morning." He shook his head in obvious disgust. "They even followed me into the market!"

"Since then I've been doing all his grocery shopping for him," Jasmine said to Cynthia, a worried look on her face.

"I'm beginning to feel like a prisoner in my own home," Tom added.

"So is Sally Ann . . ." Cynthia started to say, but decided to change the topic so as not to stir up passions. Jasmine and the twins strolled off, back to their own yard.

"How is your work going?" Cynthia said.

Tom frowned, his mood shifting as they began discussing his work. "I'm still trying to get through chapter eight of the book I'm working on now. I've had Jasmine research almost all of San Francisco and the surrounding area now, in the hopes that would give me some ideas on where to set and how to execute some of the pivotal chase scenes and action at the end, but . . ."

Cynthia felt his frustration. "It isn't working?" As the breeze died down, she became more aware of the tantalizing sage and citrus of his cologne. And then, more aware of the man himself.

In khaki walking shorts and an oversize white, short-sleeved jersey, Tom looked incredibly, ruggedly handsome. Whereas she, still in the same black suit and white silk shirt she'd worn to work, felt overdressed. The professional demeanor of her clothing was no shield against her growing feelings for, and reaction to, Tom. Nor did it seem to do much good to deter him from talking to her as if she were not just Ryan's guardian, but a personal friend.

Was she compromising herself professionally by letting him get so close to her, and vice versa? Yet how could she be expected to make a valid recommendation in regard to Ryan's custody unless she knew his father very well, and Sally Ann, too?

Tom gave a heartfelt sigh. "The problem is I can't keep my mind on the book. There are just too many interruptions. Too much going on with the case right now for me to concentrate."

"What do you mean?" she asked, both puzzled and alarmed by his grim look, and the sudden nagging feeling she'd been kept in the dark about something important.

He started, as if realizing he'd said something he shouldn't have, then deliberately evaded with a brusque, "Never mind."

Determined to find out what was going on, she moved nearer, closing the distance between them. "Tom, is there something I should know about?" she persisted bluntly, her voice no louder than a whisper, but very strong.

He hesitated, a tortured look in his blue eyes.

"Does it have to do with Ryan?" she prodded.

Again, he weighed whether or not he should confide in her. "In a way it does," he said at last. His voice dropping, he finally confided, "My agent called me a couple of days ago." Tom's eyes glimmered with sudden anger. In a sarcastic undertone, he continued, keeping his voice low so Ryan, playing nearby, wouldn't hear. "He said *Personalities* had an offer for me. They said they would give me the exact same deal they gave Sally Ann—fifteen thousand dollars for seven weeks' exclusive rights to my side of the custody case." His voice dropped another damning notch. "Photos of me and Ryan at home would have to be provided, of course."

Cynthia was filled with a sudden tension. She knew from the way Tom glanced down at her that he was aware of it, too. "What are you saying?" she whispered hoarsely.

Tom's blue eyes darkened. "I'm saying," he said, spelling it out through gritted teeth, "that Sally Ann obviously knew exactly what she was doing when she told her side of the story to *Personalities*. That she wasn't so much taken advantage of, as taking advantage." His sensual lips thinned into an aggravated line as he asked, "Didn't you ever wonder how she got the money to buy all those new toys for Ryan? And she just got another new car." He stopped and shook his head. "The idea that she would sell my son out for the sake of making a buck...." It was too despicable to be true.

Cynthia couldn't believe it. She'd known about the car, but Sally Ann had simply explained she had been able to get a bank loan. She hadn't said anything about receiving money from *Personalities*.

"And that's not all," Tom continued. "I've had a private investigator looking into her past." Ignoring Cynthia's startled look, he said, "She has a history of financial troubles. In fact, she had so much debt at one point that she had to go to a financial counselor to keep from declaring bankruptcy. It took her almost three years to repay all she had charged, and yet a couple of years later she went out and did exactly the same thing."

"She's not in debt now, though," Cynthia said, "except for the car loan she told me about."

"No, she's not," Tom admitted, his frustration and worry evident. "But how long will her prudence last, I wonder? I don't want Ryan learning to live beyond his means, thinking that it's all right. Because it's not."

Cynthia saw he had a point. But she also had been aware from her many conversations with Sally Ann that she had had financial difficulties in the past. She just hadn't told Tom about it. "I know all about Sally Ann's problems with debt," she said finally, ignoring his betrayed, faintly incredulous look. "We've talked about it at length," Cynthia continued, refusing to let Tom make her feel guilty for keeping a professional confidence. For Ryan's sake, for the sake of keeping the court battle from getting too ugly, she went on to explain the reasons behind what he already knew. "She had an impoverished childhood, Tom. That being the case, it's not so surprising that she might overspend at first and then regret it. At least she did something about it." Many people didn't. Or they took the easy way out and declared bankruptcy.

"Yeah, she did." Tom grudgingly gave her that, then went on to counter gruffly, "But there are other things she can't undo so easily—like putting our situation on the front page of *Personalities* magazine. I'm getting more offers every day for the rights to my story. That probably means she is, too. We both know, for Ryan's sake, I won't go to the press. But we have no assurances at all she won't."

Cynthia swallowed. Although they had taken steps to insure it wouldn't be that way, she had the feeling it was going to get ugly, despite all the warnings and court orders. Very ugly before all was said and done.

She didn't know what to say to Tom that would help, and for several moments they faced one another in truculent silence. Finally, she gave him what little reassurance she could. "I know Judge Mitchum. I've worked with him in the past. He bends over backward to be fair to people, and as a devoted father himself he's especially sympathetic in custody cases." She was about to say he just had to trust, when he interrupted her.

"Meaning what?" Tom asked, troubled. "That you think he'll rule in my favor?"

She knew he needed, wanted, her to reassure him as any friend would, but she couldn't discuss what Judge Mitchum might or might not do for Tom.

The truth was at that point she wasn't even sure what her recommendation would be. She was leaning toward some type of joint-custody agreement that would benefit all three people, and give Ryan the optimum chance to be loved. Not about to say that to Tom, though, without hurting his feelings or compromising herself professionally, she said only, "I think he'll be fair, that's all." She swallowed hard and then finished what she'd been trying to get out earlier, before he'd interrupted. "You just have to have faith everything will work out for the best."

From the way he looked at her she had the feeling they were light-years apart, that he couldn't have been less a fatalist if he tried. He shook his head in obvious regret. "I just wish it were that simple."

She had the feeling he was talking about a lot more than Sally Ann or Ryan. She had the feeling he was talking about them, too, and she knew she could do nothing about that situation.

Chapter Ten

"I agree, something has to be done," Judge Mitchum said, as he looked at the copy of the *National Tattletale* in front of him. On the front page was a color photo of Tom roughly escorting an intrusive photographer from his backyard, while the twins and a wide-eyed Jasmine looked on. The caption read: Stress Getting to Surrogate Dad as He Awaits Court Trial Next Week.

Cynthia had cringed when she read it; she could only imagine how disabused and violated Tom felt.

"The article makes me sound like I'm about to flip out," Tom told the judge.

Sally Ann frowned and added, "I've been having trouble, too, Judge. The reporters are everywhere. I can't even take a coffee break at the hospital anymore without one of them popping out at me, asking questions."

"Well, maybe the best thing is for you all to get out of town for the weekend," Judge Mitchum said. "Sally Ann?"

"I guess I could go visit my sister in Amarillo," she said.

"I think that'd be wise," he agreed.

"I could go to Galveston," Tom said. "Ryan would probably enjoy the beach."

"Just be sure and be back for court first thing Tuesday morning," Judge Mitchum cautioned. He gave them an additional warning to try to remain cool during the coming proceedings for Ryan's sake, and then dismissed them.

I ought to feel relieved, Cynthia thought as she left the chambers. *I won't have to deal with any of this all weekend.* But as Friday night wore on, she couldn't seem to stop thinking about Tom. Maybe because he still had Ryan with him, and because he more than anyone had been the target of persistent reporters.

What if one of them had followed him to his weekend getaway, despite all the precautions he'd promised Judge Mitchum he would take? What if he lost his temper with one of then? What if a reporter accidentally scared or hurt Ryan, in his zeal to get an exclusive?

By Saturday morning, Cynthia knew she would have no peace unless she found out for herself that Ryan and Tom were doing all right, so she called his father in Houston. "Tom didn't give me a number, but I figured you would know how to reach him."

"I sure do," Tom Sr. replied kindly. "And I'll be glad to give it to you, along with the address, although you don't need to worry about Tom being alone down there. Toby Williams went down to keep him company."

Cynthia couldn't think of a worse person for Tom or Ryan to be with at the present time. She'd never forget the last time she'd seen him, hopping out of that stretch limo, a scantily dressed femme fatale on each arm—one of whom had been meant for Tom. She closed her eyes, aware of a sudden pounding in her temples and a tumultuous churning in her middle.

"Toby was worried about Tom, too. Said he was going to take a group of friends and go see him, try to get Tom's mind off the upcoming trial next week."

His father's words hit her like a blow. She sat down, not liking any of the pictures that came to mind. A short while later she was on the road to Galveston.

"CYNTHIA, WHAT ARE YOU doing here?" Tom cried, his eyes narrowing. He held her gaze in a way that made it impossible for her to look away. "Nothing's wrong is it? Nothing's happened?"

"No." She lifted her chin a notch and attempted to appear cool and professional, exactly the opposite of the way she felt. When her taxi from the airport had pulled up to Tom's beach condominium, she had watched Toby and a pair of buxom blondes pull away in a stretch limo.

The blue of his eyes darkened. His expression became more puzzled. "Then why...?"

"I'm here to make a spot check."

"Yeah, great."

His sarcasm stung; but she decided to ignore it. "May I see Ryan?"

"Sure. He's upstairs asleep." Tom pointed in the right direction. "First bedroom on your right."

Cynthia nodded, and aware of his eyes upon her, made her way up the stairs. When she came back down, Tom was waiting for her, his arms crossed over his chest. "Everything okay?"

He knew it was. She nodded, feeling stupid now for having worried so very much. She kept her voice light, matter-of-fact. "He's out like a light. He must've had quite a day."

"He did. Toby's great with kids. The women took a turn entertaining him, in fact."

The women.... Reminded of why she'd come, she took note of every shred of evidence in the living room. There were plenty of glasses around, but to her embarrassed chagrin, all were filled with the last drops of cola or iced tea. There didn't appear to be a drop of liquor in the house. His party appeared to have been of the most mundane, innocent sort.

"You don't trust Toby, do you?" said Tom. "You don't trust me when I'm with him."

She hadn't meant to be that transparent. But now that he had brought the subject up, she decided to pursue it. "It's true. I was worried about what I'd find here."

"Do you really think I'd jeopardize Ryan's emotional and physical well-being for any reason?" he asked in a husky voice. Not giving her a chance to answer, he continued tersely, "Toby came down here because he knew I was upset."

"About the article in the *National Tattletale*?"

"It's more than that. It's the hearing next week. It's everything." His voice caught abruptly and he whirled away from her. He stalked out onto the screened-in back porch and stood with hands in his pockets, staring out at the ocean. After a long silence, he said in a low voice underscored with anguish, "I'm afraid I'm going to lose custody of Ryan. And I don't know if I can handle that."

Watching him struggle with his feelings, Cynthia felt her throat close up. She hated to see people in pain, and seeing Tom so close to breaking down was especially difficult. She swallowed hard, fighting to keep her own emotions under tight control. She had to be neutral here, apart, and yet she wanted to comfort him...

Oblivious to her thoughts, Tom continued in a low raspy voice, "Last night, I started thinking about what would happen if I did lose, if I no longer had Ryan in my life."

Her breath caught and she moved closer. She could see the tears streaming freely down his face.

Hoarsely, Tom continued, "I started thinking about what it would be like to get up in the morning and not hear him in his crib, calling for me to come and get him out of there. Or fix him breakfast while the coffee's brewing. To not have to pick up his toys dozens of times each day, or stay up all night with him when he's teething or sick. I started thinking about Christmas and his birthday and all the plans I had for him, the vacations I wanted to take, the ball games I wanted us to go see.

"I thought about the times when he's really needed me to be there for him, like when he goes to the doctor for a shot or has a nightmare in the middle of the night or is sick and doesn't understand why he feels so lousy—he just knows he wants his daddy to hold him.

And I started wondering what it would be like if I wasn't there for him. Would he ever understand why I wasn't there? Would he ever forgive me, or would he always end up feeling betrayed and unwanted and unloved, as if I had deliberately pushed him away? And how in hell is anyone going to explain this to him at his age if the judge does take him away from me—my lawyer says it is a distinct possibility, one I have to prepare for. How is he going to be able to cope?'' Tom's voice hardened with anger and fear.

Cynthia didn't have the answers for that. No one did.

She touched his arm, dimly aware that tears of anguish were running down her face now, too. She didn't want to even think of Ryan or Tom in pain, and yet she knew what he had just described might happen. ''You have to believe that somehow this is all going to work out—no matter what the judge decides.''

He turned to her, his expression brooding and bleak. ''I wish it were that simple,'' he said heavily, his voice devoid of hope.

''It is.'' It had to be.

''Is it?'' Sliding a hand underneath her chin, he forced her face up, so she had no choice but to look at him, to face the cold reality of the situation ahead of them. ''I wish I could believe that, Cynthia, but every time I look at you I'm reminded how tenuous everything in life is, how fragile.'' His eyelids lowering, he traced the salty path of her tears with the pad of his thumb. ''And that only makes me want to hold on to the things near and dear to me all the tighter. It makes me want to risk.'' His fingers moved from the underside of her chin, to the nape of her neck, the shift both languorous and erotic, and then slowly, ever so slowly, with the same certain skill, his mouth lowered to hers.

She saw the kiss coming. She knew she should resist. But something stronger than the premonition of wrongness, of danger, held her riveted in place. When his lips touched hers, any thought she might have had of fleeing vanished.

She had waited for this day forever, it seemed. And now that it was here, she couldn't get enough of him, nor he of her. Over and over his lips skimmed hers, touching, evoking, making her feel wanted. Exquisite pleasure billowed up deep inside her. His kisses got deeper, more demanding still. Unable to get enough of him, she held him more tightly, her arms wrapped around his powerful shoulders, her breasts pressed against his chest. And still it wasn't enough. She wanted them to melt together, body and soul, until she no longer knew where her body ended and his began. And it was only when his hand reached for the buttons at the neck of her blouse that she regained her senses.

As much as she wanted, needed, for him to touch her and love her, this was wrong. She couldn't let it happen. Not now, no matter how much she wanted it to. With the heels of both hands, she pushed him away. "No, Tom . . ." He released her and she pivoted away, her body still thrumming and aching, her heart and mind bereft. Unable to bear it, she began for the door.

He caught her arm and gently reeled her in. "I need you," he said, one arm sliding around her waist.

I need you, too. I need this. But it's wrong!

She knew if she looked into his eyes again, she would be lost. She kept her head down, her gaze riveted on his lower chest. Oh God, she didn't want to do this, didn't want to say no, but she had to. "I am Ryan's guardian," she recited with stony resolve, wishing fervently she weren't so aware of him next to her, or the warmth of his touch, or the way her body still pulsed and burned, the way her heart yearned. But none of that mattered now and they both knew it. "I have to make a recommendation about the custody next week," she finished on an anguished note.

At the reminder, whatever joy he'd felt, whatever desire, faded, and Tom's body stilled. He let her go, sparing her the obvious question. She closed her eyes, her whole being sagging with relief, her heart aching in a way that couldn't be assuaged.

They didn't speak again as she went inside and called a cab. She'd never known a more intense loneliness.

ALL DAY SUNDAY, and late into Monday, Cynthia was filled with guilt over what had happened. She knew the self-chastising would not help, however, and to get her mind off herself, she decided to concentrate on her mother's problems. Unfortunately her efforts in that regard were not met with glee.

"You brought someone over here now?" Faith asked her incredulously, late Monday afternoon.

Cynthia wasn't the least bit deterred by her mother's look of unappreciation. She walked over to open the curtains, and sunlight poured into the dusty room. "Yes," she answered her mother calmly. "A high-school student, and she's waiting in the car, so you'd better hurry."

"Cynthia, I can't see anyone this afternoon."

"Sure you can," Cynthia said, not about to give an inch now that her latest plan to get her mother back in action was in motion. "Just get dressed."

Her mother stood up slowly and squared her shoulders. "Let me put it another way," her mother said, firmly enunciating each and every word. "I won't see anyone."

Their strong wills had been put to the test. Determined to be the victor this once, Cynthia countered archly, "Oh, yes, you will, Mother. Dressed or not. Now which is it going to be?" She stood facing her mom, her hands on her hips.

Faith frowned. "You have a lot of nerve."

Cynthia grinned. "It's inherited." Sobering slightly, she said softly, "I also have a high-school student in the car who, from what I understand, is magnificently talented but unable to get over her recurring stage fright." Cynthia paused, letting her words sink in. She could tell by the instantly sympathetic look on her mother's face that she was already interested. More persuasively, Cynthia added, "She needs help, Mother. And as you were always such a wonderful performer, so at ease in front of an audience, you're exactly the one to give it."

For a moment Faith was silent, frowning and thinking. "I wasn't always that way, you know," she said finally.

"You can tell her that, too," Cynthia said gently, pointing in the direction of Faith's bedroom. "Now, come on. Hurry up. Or she's going to think I've all but forgotten her," Cynthia said, peering out the window.

"All right, I'm going," Faith grumbled, "for the child's sake."

As she had hoped, her mother's session with the student was of enormous help to them both. Before the student had left, she'd learned several relaxation techniques to use when she was practicing, as well as performing. She'd also signed up for another session. Cynthia knew once word was out others would follow.

She took the student home, then, realizing her mother still wanted to talk to her, returned to Faith's home. Faith was waiting for her. "That was a dirty rotten trick," her mother started the moment Cynthia walked in the door. Now that the student was gone, she seemed more depressed than ever.

Cynthia's spirits sank. She had been so sure this was the key to her mother's recovery. Realizing she had to tread carefully now, she said, "I know you have every right to be furious with me, but I can't stand watching you just wither away."

Faith's eyes welled with tears behind the oversize lenses. Her voice was whisper-thin when she spoke. "How do you think I feel, not being able to play the way I used to?"

Cynthia embraced her mother and hugged her tightly. Her eyes were wet, too, when they parted. "You still have a lot to give, Mom," Cynthia said when she found her voice again. "Whether you ever regain full use of your hand and your playing ability or not, you still have tons of knowledge. You can conduct master classes and give lessons on stage presence and heaven only knows what else.''

''Cynthia, to do that adequately, a teacher has to play! I know you meant well, but this just isn't going to work. Now if you don't mind, I'm tired. I'd really like to rest.''

The discussion was closed.

CYNTHIA DROVE HOME, more depressed than ever. It seemed everything was going wrong. And with Ryan's custody trial due to begin tomorrow, she didn't see how it was going to get any better. Changing into navy shorts and a matching blouse, she heated a frozen dinner in the microwave, then settled down to make her final preparations for the trial.

All the paperwork had been prepared the week before, of course. All she had to do now was go over her own notes for the judge, and read through the written evaluations of the psychologist and social worker she'd enlisted to aid in her decision.

Unfortunately, no one agreed on any one custody arrangement, which left Cynthia feeling as torn and mixed up as ever as she put everything away at nine o'clock. She knew what she was going to do, she thought, assuming nothing changed between now and the time she was to testify. Nevertheless, it was a difficult decision, one that she felt would haunt her for years to come.

Deciding she needed to relax, she turned on the stereo; the record had just started when her doorbell rang.

Pausing only long enough to turn down the stereo, Cynthia padded barefoot to the door. She was stunned to see Tom Harrigan on the other side of it. In khaki slacks and a wine colored polo shirt, he was devastatingly handsome.

Swallowing hard around the sudden knot of tension in her throat, she said, "You shouldn't be here."

Not waiting for an invitation, he pushed past her and stepped into the cozy ambience of her yellow-and-white living room, his tall figure looking impossibly masculine and daunting amidst the Laura Ashley prints. "I had to see you," he said quietly, turning to face her.

Exactly what she'd been afraid of. Cynthia shut the front door and remained where she was, leaning against it. "Tom, please," she said raggedly, shutting her eyes. "Don't do this." *Don't say anymore. Don't make me change my mind about you. And about Ryan.*

"I can't help it, Cynthia." He came back toward her slowly, his eyes holding hers. "I have to know if what happened Saturday night is going to count against me."

Had it been just Saturday? It seemed a lifetime ago that he had kissed her, and it seemed a second ago, the memory was that real.

He stopped when he was a scant six inches away. Aware that the pulse in her neck was jumping, she kept her gaze fastened on his neck. "If you're referring to the fact you were upset when we talked, forget it. You were entitled."

He stepped closer still. His hands came up to cup her shoulders gently. "I'm referring to the fact I kissed you."

His voice was as soft and beguiling as velvet, but she refused to let it soften her. Moving easily out of his light grip, she said stiffly, "If you're here to say you're sorry—" she was hanging on to her composure by a thread "—apology accepted."

He grinned rapaciously. "I'm not."

Help me, she thought. *Someone help me.* "Then why are you here?" she asked crisply.

His eyes darkened to a midnight blue, and for a moment the two of them were silent.

"You want the truth?"

"Yes." *I think.*

"I'm here," he said softly, his hands slipping around her waist, "to see if it was as good as I thought, as good as I remember. As real. I meant what I said the other night, Cynthia," he whispered huskily, drawing her nearer still. "I need you. I never realized until this moment how much."

He pulled her into his embrace. All the longings she'd felt for him, all the pent-up emotions of the past three months hit her with tidal-wave force. She wanted to be with him. It was that simple. And that complicated.

She was tired of the struggle, the problems, only seeing the pain in life. She yearned to see the hope and know the pleasure, and she knew in the deepest recesses of her heart he could give that to her. Maybe it was wrong of her to take this, she thought, but it would be wronger still to deny them this one chance, perhaps the only chance they would ever have....

"Cynthia," he murmured, lifting both his hands to frame her face with a deliberateness that stole the breath from her lungs. She felt her legs weaken and heard herself sigh, the sound faraway and indistinct, and then his mouth was on hers again, and it was as if the earth had stopped, as if there was nothing else in the world except the two of them, and this moment in time.

His lips moved down her throat, the frissons of pleasure his kisses created making her arch her neck and spine. He pushed her shirt up, so they could touch skin to skin, and still the kisses continued—deep, endless, penetrating communications from heart and soul.

She'd thought she'd known what it was to make love with a man, to give everything she had to give; she hadn't. She'd thought she'd known about passion; but she hadn't. She'd thought she'd known about love, how deep and satisfying and soul-quenching it could be. But she hadn't, not until he touched her, not until he kissed her, not until he telegraphed with his body exactly what he wanted.

And then she knew. This was how exquisite it could be.

Between kisses and caresses, they undressed one another with abandon. Outside was the darkness of night and the uncertainty of the world, but inside, all was cozy, safe. Her breath shuddered out as he kissed the corners of her mouth and then he followed her down onto the floor, their clothes a tangled bed beneath them. She opened her arms to him; she opened her heart. He took solace where he found it, giving everything she offered back tenfold. And when it was over, they clung together mindlessly, quietly, their heartbeats slowing gradually.

He raised up on one elbow to look at her. "I'm sorry," he said, brushing the hair from her face. "I never meant... That wasn't very comfortable for you, was it?"

She hadn't even noticed the hardness of the floor, only the taut musculature of his body pressed against hers, the urgency, the warmth. The truth was he had taken her breath away, and just looking at him now, she wanted him again in the same all-consuming way. Was this part of their relationship destined? she wondered. Could she afford to let it go on?

Suddenly, she just felt confused. She cared about him deeply, but she was still responsible for what happened to his son. And ultimately to him. It was a burden she now didn't want to bear, but she knew she must if this custody case were ever to be resolved.

Needing to distance herself from the tantalizing invitation in his look, she sat up and reached for her blouse, pulling it on, covering herself. A puzzled, faintly hurt look in his eyes, he followed suit and got dressed, too.

"I wish I could resign as Ryan's guardian," she began, afraid to look at him, really look at him for fear she would dissolve in his arms once again if she did. "But I can't, because to do so would mean they'd have to appoint someone else and the evaluation process would start all over again. They'd have to set another court date. It would be months before this was ever resolved."

Tom was pensive now, too. "You're saying you're sorry we made love, is that it?" he asked quietly.

At that moment, Cynthia wanted nothing more than to lose herself in his arms and block out everything else but this moment, this man, the special feelings she had found just in being with him. But she couldn't do that. She had to think about Ryan first and how none of this, not any of it, would affect the decision she had already made on Ryan's behalf.

"Yes," she said honestly, "I am sorry, because it was wrong. It shouldn't have happened."

"Now, or at all?"

She could see his face, and feel his anger, his frustration. He moved away from her slightly, and then unexpectedly his mood gentled.

"When I was a kid," he said softly, his low voice underscoring every word, "my brother Mike got hit by a car and almost died. I learned then how precious life is, that we mustn't take anything—or anyone—for granted. Life is precious, Cynthia. Too precious to waste." He waited a heartbeat. "You'd do well to remember that," he said softly.

And on that warning note, he left. Cynthia wanted to stop him, but for his sake and for Ryan's, she knew she couldn't. Whatever would or would not happen between them would have to wait until after the custody case was resolved. There was no other way for either of them.

Chapter Eleven

"Before we go to the courthouse, there's something your mother and I want to talk to you about," Tom Sr. said early Tuesday morning.

"Go ahead," Tom said, although he had an idea from the look on his father's face he wasn't going to like what he had to say.

"We've been giving your situation a lot of thought. Sally Ann stated her case very poignantly in that magazine article. A lot of people still think motherhood is sacred, something not to be denied anyone, without reasonable cause."

"Dad, she couldn't have cared less about him for the first year of his life!" If that wasn't reasonable cause, he didn't know what was!

Tom Sr. was silent as he exchanged a tentative look with his wife. "We know that, son. But she's had a change of heart now, and Ryan has accepted her as his mother. We have to think about what the judge is going to say, about what's happened in other cases like this..."

Tom swore mentally and counted to ten. His parents' timing couldn't have been worse. He didn't need this on the day of the hearing. Fighting to keep a lid on his temper, he said slowly, "There haven't been any cases like this, Dad, where the mother changed her mind a year later. All the cases in dispute have been about mothers who changed their minds right after the baby was born, before anyone really had a chance to bond."

"Right, and in all but one, the baby was given back to the mother. Fair or not, that might happen here," his father continued.

"And we couldn't bear to see that happen," Rachel cut in. She paused, emotion shimmering in her eyes. "We don't want to see you lose Ryan altogether. And the experts we consulted think that might happen unless you and Sally Ann both put your own needs aside and come to some sort of compromise on your own before this case gets to court and the outcome is taken out of your hands and put into the court's." She took a deep breath. "Think about it, Tom. Think about what it could mean for all of you if you settled this matter privately, rather than dragged Ryan and yourselves through the publicity. It's bound to get ugly if it continues. We don't think you want that for Ryan."

Tom didn't, either, but nor was he willing to give up sole custody of Ryan.

"What are you saying?" he asked slowly, angry that his parents were not supporting him now—now when he needed them most.

"We think you ought to consider settling for joint custody, instead of going ahead with the fight for full custody."

As the impact of his dad's words sank in, he stared at his parents incredulously. "I can't believe you're asking me to give up now." They had always told him anything was possible, if he set his heart and his mind to it, and they had been right. Now they were asking him to become a quitter, and at the most crucial point in his life, no less. He stared at them, hurt and bewildered by their sudden change of attitude.

They seemed to know how he felt, too. "Tom, we're only thinking of you and Ryan," his mother said emotionally, just as he was getting ready to argue.

"Maybe so, but you're wrong," he volleyed back.

"Are we?" Rachel surprised him with the depth of her conviction. "Sally Ann is Ryan's mother, and because of that she has a right to be a part of his life, just the way you do."

Tom knew that now; he hadn't a couple of months ago. "I'm not disputing that fact, Mom," he said with as much patience as he could muster, "but Ryan needs one home, not two." On that he was going to stand firm. "I'll allow Sally Ann as much visitation as we can reasonably work in, but Ryan belongs with me. And that's the way it's going to stay."

His parents were silent. They apparently knew now they hadn't a prayer of changing his mind on this, and so were not going to argue the point further. The strained silence continued for several more moments before his mother finally spoke again. "Do you have any idea of what Ryan's guardian is going to say in court, what arrangement she favors?" Rachel asked quietly.

Tom shook his head numbly. He wished he did know what Cynthia was going to say when she got up on the stand.

SHE HADN'T THOUGHT it was going to be this hard. Cynthia steeled herself as she took a seat in the courtroom. Tom's whole family was assembled in there. Sally Ann had a few people from the hospital where she worked, and a lot more supporters who'd read about the case.

As the hearing started and Sally Ann took the stand, she began to tell in her own words why she had agreed to bear a child for Tom. The tension in the room only increased. "I thought I was doing something noble," she said, her voice quivering slightly, her hands folded demurely in her lap. "I knew how much he wanted a child and I wanted to help."

"It didn't occur to you how painful it would be, giving your own child up?" her attorney, Myron Singleton, asked.

"I put it from my mind," she said, her eyes filling with tears. "But when I saw him that day, I knew...I knew I couldn't deny him any longer, and that's when I decided to sue for joint custody."

Cynthia took a deep breath. She could see Tom. He looked tense and unhappy.

"You're saying, then, that it wasn't the money driving you to accept the terms of the agreement?" her attorney pressed.

"No," Sally Ann said softly.

"What was it then?"

There was silence as Sally Ann darted a look at Tom and then promptly dropped her eyes, as if intimidated by him even now. "It was Tom Harrigan, the way he pressured me. He can be a very charming man and he...kept telling me over and over how much he wanted a baby, how he couldn't have one any other way." Tears filled her eyes and she had difficulty continuing. "I've always wanted to help people, that's why I became a nurse...."

"You're telling the court he pressured you to cooperate?"

Her tone turned accusing. "He seemed to know I have a hard time saying no to people. That's why he insisted on all those informal meetings away from the lawyers, with just the two of us. He said he wanted to get to know me, but I realize now it was just to convince me to do things his way, to make me feel like I'd be doing the baby irreparable harm if I ever tried to have any contact with the child at all—"

Tom's lawyer jumped to her feet. "I object, your honor!" It was all Tom could do to contain himself. Sally Ann at this point was pitiful.

"Overruled," Judge Mitchum said. "Mr. Harrigan will have his turn to tell his side of the story."

Tom's lawyer sat down reluctantly, as Tom glared at Sally Ann. When they broke for a short recess, Tom pulled Cynthia into a private conference room, through the crush of reporters.

"She's lying through her teeth," Tom said fiercely. "I never coerced her in any way." He shook his head in bewilderment, obviously dismayed by the turn of events. "I thought because she was an RN and had borne another surrogate child without consequence that she knew what she was getting into, that there was no chance she'd ever renege."

Her mind swimming with confusion, Cynthia advised, "You've got to calm down. If you operate in a temper, it'll work against you."

To Cynthia's dismay, the rest of the afternoon went just as badly as the morning. Sally Ann painted a picture of herself as a victim, who'd been too naive for her own good, while Tom—helpless to defend himself at that point—got angrier and angrier. By the time Tom's lawyer got up to cross-examine Sally Ann, she was out for blood. And Tom seemed to take delight in the unmerciful way she got it. "You're asking us to believe you care for your son, more than anything in this world, yet at the first possible opportunity you violated the court-ordered secrecy surrounding this case and sold his story to a magazine!"

Sally Ann seemed to shrink even farther into her seat on the witness stand. "They were going to print it anyway."

"Tom Harrigan didn't find it necessary to profit from his son's pain. But you did, and what that says about your ability to mother this child is very unsettling indeed."

Sally Ann's lawyer objected. Sally Ann burst into tears. Court was adjourned briefly, only to be resumed later as Tom's lawyer conducted a merciless examination of Sally Ann's financial situation, her history of indebtedness and impulsiveness.

Given what had been told in just one day, Cynthia
feared what would be brought to light when Tom was
on the stand. And she feared for Ryan, for the time
when he was old enough to understand and learn
about—perhaps cruelly, from others—what had gone
on in this custody case, how both his parents had been
belittled and defamed.

Unhappily, a visitation with Ryan and his mother
was scheduled for that very evening. En route to Tom's
house to pick up Ryan, Cynthia prayed that he had
calmed down. To her surprise, he wasn't even there.

Jasmine was. "His parents tried to get him to go out
to dinner with them, while Ryan visited with Sally Ann,
but he wouldn't hear of it. He said he wanted to be
alone, and well, after what happened in court today, I
can't blame him for wanting to get the heck away from
everything for a little while."

Cynthia knew Tom and his lawyer had done their
own share of mud slinging. To the point where she,
too, wasn't sure any of this was ever going to be worth
it. "Is he playing tennis?" Cynthia asked, slinging
Ryan's diaper bag over her arm. Although she had
promised herself to retain her objectivity during the
remainder of this case, she still cared about Tom, and
couldn't help but ask about him.

"No, he was too wound up, too angry, to do even
that," Jasmine said. She watched as Cynthia picked up
Ryan and carried the toddler out the front door.
"You're going to be at your house, as usual?" Cyn-
thia nodded. "Well, I'll let him know you picked up
Ryan on schedule when he gets back."

"Thanks."

As Cynthia expected, Sally Ann was equally upset. She felt the hearing was slanted unfairly against her. "I wasn't trying to make Tom look bad," she told Cynthia in a shaking voice that held the first traces of panic. She swallowed hard, getting control of herself once again. "I just wanted the judge to understand why I acted as I did, how I got talked into this in the first place." She shuddered. "Did you see the way Tom looked at me? He looked like he wanted to have me hung upside down from the nearest lamppost."

Cynthia agreed. If Tom were to encounter Sally Ann just now, God only knew what he would do in his current emotional state.

"Look, Sally Ann, tempers are running high just now. I think the best thing for you to do is just try to keep a low profile, especially around Tom and his family, and I will try to get Tom and his family to do the same. My main concern—and yours, too—has to be Ryan. We don't want him upset by all this."

Sally Ann nodded, looking soberly at her son. "I guess you're right. I don't want to hurt my baby."

As the next few days passed, Cynthia noted that the courtroom only grew more tense. Sally Ann's attorney tried to paint Tom as a fun-loving bachelor, similar to the reckless debonair hero in his spy novels, whereas Tom's attorney focused on Tom's stability as a parent, his devotedness to Ryan, his rosy financial outlook. Sally Ann's financial outlook couldn't begin to compare with Tom's and Tom's lawyer made quite sure everyone knew this.

Unfortunately, it was Myron Singleton, Sally Ann's lawyer, who had the last word. "I agree the different economic levels between the two households could be confusing for a child. However, the financial disparity could be lessened by support payments from Mr. Harrigan. There is, of course, no replacing the loving care only a mother can give her child...."

Support payments! Cynthia thought, alarm bells sounding in her head. No one had ever said anything about support. Sally Ann looked equally upset. Tom was livid.

He lambasted his lawyer as soon as court was adjourned for the day. "I've put up with a lot the past few months, but I'll be damned if I'm paying her support money on top of everything else! I've already paid in blood."

Sally Ann pulled Cynthia aside. "Asking for support was not my idea," she began frantically. "I didn't even know Tom had the kind of money he does until today, when his lawyers started throwing out those figures."

"What do you mean?" Cynthia asked.

"He never told me that he was a bestselling author, that he had a famous father, or anything. I mean, I knew he was a writer at the time I signed the surrogacy agreement, but that was all."

"You had no idea he was famous in his own right?" Cynthia was stunned.

"No. How could I have, when he writes under a pen name? Not that I read much beside professional publications and magazines, anyway. I assumed he wrote for magazines."

"He told you that?" Cynthia asked, her disbelief showing in her face.

She nodded. "Yes, when we first met. I wanted to know what he did for a living and he told me he was a writer. He said he'd had articles published in *Sports Illustrated* several years before that. Said he was currently working on longer book-length stuff. He was very vague, and frankly, since it all had to do with sports, I wasn't interested."

"So you let it drop?" Cynthia felt sick inside. The picture Sally Ann was painting went against everything she thought she knew about Tom.

"I was more concerned about his aptitude for parenthood, making sure he really wanted a child and would care for him or her." She paused, reflecting. "He deliberately misled me, didn't he? About what the rest of his life had really been like? I mean, I remember him mentioning he had a solid family base, that his sister was a teacher, his brother a psychologist, and that his parents lived in Houston, but that was about all. I didn't have any idea he was anyone more prominent until Myron Singleton mentioned it in passing several weeks after I'd legally asked for custody. I guess he just assumed I knew, as I guess I should have," she finished slowly. "It wasn't right for him to lie to me like that, was it?" She looked at Cynthia for confirmation.

Cynthia felt ripped in two. This was getting so complicated, so confusing. She didn't know whose side she should be on, save Ryan's, and because she cared about Tom, she was beginning to feel terribly uncomfortable.

Would the same happen to Ryan? Would he feel as torn as she did? How would he cope? As a child, how could he be expected to? Unfortunately, she had no answers to those questions, and she didn't feel they would be forthcoming anytime soon; she just knew she had to talk to Tom and hear his side of the story.

When court resumed, Tom was put on the stand. When asked if he had deliberately misrepresented himself to Sally Ann he sighed and admitted tensely, "Everything I told her was the truth. I just didn't tell her everything."

Disappointment cut into Cynthia like a knife.

As if sensing the disappointment in the courtroom, he continued gruffly, "I was afraid if she knew about my background, the fact I come from such a prominent family, that she'd try to pull something like what just happened back in that courtroom." His blue eyes clouded with anger.

"Has that kind of thing happened before?" his attorney asked.

He nodded and said with great bitterness, "Yes, this has happened to me, more times than I care to remember." His voice was harsh. "People would want to get close to me at school. I'd find out later it was only because my father was a professional ball player. Then later, when he retired from sports and became a sports announcer, it was the same thing all over again. My college fraternity elected me entertainment chairman. It turned out later they'd only done it because they expected that I could get free passes to all the Astro games and permission to enter the team locker room. Stuff like that. Maybe I should've expected it, but I never did. I wanted to be liked for me, and most of the time I was. But any time my father's profession, his celebrity came into things, everything seemed to get all screwed up again, bent out of shape.'' He released another long sigh as he struggled for the words to explain. ''People act differently when they step into the limelight. They do things they wouldn't otherwise think about, because they get starstruck. I know that. I've lived it. That's why I chose from the very beginning to write under a pen name and live a low-profile life. Yes, I occasionally go out on tour for a book, but it's as Harrison James. At home, I'm just Tom, a writer who labors at his work like anyone else in any other profession. Yes, there are a few perks, but also hardships— the time I have to spend alone to get my writing done, for one thing, the ups and downs of the publishing world, for another. But I'm not a celebrity at home, I'm not a star and I don't try to be. I do my own laundry, like everybody else. I do my own cooking, my own cleaning.'' He let out his breath slowly as he vented the last of his exasperation. Calming slightly, he ran a hand through his hair and said in a much softer, more penitent voice, ''If I was vague when I described what it was I did for a living in my talks with Sally Ann, it was only because I didn't want the financial aspects of things, my fame—past or present—coming in to muck things up. I didn't want her doing this for me because of who I am, or what I might become in the future, or because she wanted to have a child who was grandchild to a former pro baseball player, or related by blood to the famous Harrigan clan.''

''And you think she might have wanted to have a child by you for that reason?'' Myron Singleton pressed.

"Or for my trust fund," Tom allowed pointedly.

Myron grinned like a Cheshire cat. "You live well?"

"On what I make," Tom acknowledged defensively. He gave Sally Ann a smoldering look that made her squirm and lower her head. "I've never touched my trust fund and I don't intend to. The money in it is for Ryan when he comes of age," Tom finished firmly, glaring at Sally Ann. "As for support—" he sucked in his breath again, looking very angry as he faced the judge "—I really don't feel I owe her anything on that level, under the circumstances."

Cynthia couldn't fault him for thinking that way. In his place, she wouldn't have wanted to pay child support to Sally Ann, either. Nonetheless, she worried about the way he had tried to fool Sally Ann in the first place. The fact remained, he had lied by omission, and was still defending his right to have done so.

The knowledge that he would go to any lengths to achieve what he set out to do, bothered her tremendously. It made her wonder what would happen if the custody case was not decided in his favor.

By the time court had ended for the third day, both Tom and Sally Ann looked tense and nervous, as if they knew it could go either way. Neither was willing to lose, and Tom—irritated by Sally Ann's lawyer's portrayal of him—was not willing to compromise and go for a joint-custody arrangement, either.

Cynthia's heart went out to both of them, for she knew how much they were suffering, how much they loved Ryan. In her efforts to remain impartial, though, she tried to avoid further conversations with Sally Ann and Tom as much as possible. She knew both were anxious and hurting, but she couldn't let herself get sucked into either's emotions. Her decision, as to whom custody should go to, had already been made—before she had even gone to Galveston. And that decision remained firm, even if she dreaded the day she had to take the witness stand and deliver her recommendation.

"So who are you going to recommend gets custody of Ryan?" Sally Ann asked Cynthia later that day, as she arrived at Cynthia's for her scheduled visitation with Ryan.

Cynthia concentrated on Ryan, who was toddling on back toward the spare room at Cynthia's house to show his mother his new toy. "Blocks, Mama," he said, "blocks."

"How pretty, Ryan!" Sally Ann exclaimed, bending down to give him another hug, which he returned wholeheartedly. "Did you build this tower yourself?"

Ryan shook his head and giggled mischievously.

Cynthia and Sally Ann laughed, too. Lately, Ryan said no to everything, although he had built the tower with Cynthia's help, while they waited for Sally Ann to arrive.

Because she wanted the matter closed, Cynthia said in the most subdued tone possible, "Let's not talk about the custody case, Sally Ann. Please. Let's just give it a rest." After three grueling days, she needed one. And she felt Sally Ann did, too.

The telephone rang. Cynthia excused herself and went to get it. A moment later, she returned, a perplexed look on her face. "There's a messenger at my office. He's insisting I come over and sign for a package from the IRS. Can you manage if I'm gone for fifteen minutes?" She hoped nothing was wrong with her tax return. She had filed several weeks ago. Could it be she was going to be audited?

Sally Ann shrugged. "Sure. You go on and don't worry about us." She smiled at Ryan and tenderly ruffled his hair. "We'll be fine."

Still puzzling over the package that the messenger stated could only be delivered to her work address, Cynthia arrived at her office five minutes later. Sure enough, a uniformed messenger was standing out in front of her building, a package in his hand. Cynthia glanced at the return address. "Why couldn't you have brought this to my home?"

The messenger shrugged. "Don't ask me, lady. I just follow directions, and the note on this package said: 'Deliver to office address only, as soon as possible.' You can see yourself it was dropped off at one of our locations a couple of hours ago. They paid extra to have it delivered this evening by six-thirty."

Frowning, Cynthia opened the package. Inside was a stack of unused tax forms and a brochure explaining the new tax laws. Nothing else.

"Stranger and stranger," Cynthia murmured, getting right back into her car. Was this a practical joke, or the first sign that her yearly tax return had failed to reach the IRS office, as it should have, several weeks earlier when she'd mailed it? She groaned, thinking if that were the case, she would have to file all over again.

Her bewilderment increased as she approached her house and saw the police car pulling up in front. What now? she wondered, a feeling of dread rushing through her. She hoped nothing had happened to Ryan in her absence. If it had, she would never forgive herself, and Tom wouldn't forgive her, either! Parking her car hurriedly at the curb, she leaped out and dashed up the front steps after the policeman.

Sally Ann came out of the house at a run, tears streaming down her face, an angry red welt on the left side of her jaw.

Seeing Cynthia, she began to weep even harder.

Instinctively Cynthia put her arms around her frail shoulders. The surge of panic inside her grew. "What happened?"

Sally Ann continued to sob, her voice harsh and loud in the stillness of the humid air. "As soon as you l-l-left, Tom came by." With her fingers, she wiped the tears from her cheeks. "He was furious when he found out you had gone out on an errand and left me here alone with Ryan." Her voice hitched and her shoulders began to shake convulsively.

Cynthia hugged her and waited patiently for her sobs to subside. "Then what happened?"

Sally Ann shrugged and shook her head. "He was just so angry," she whispered, closing her eyes. "I tried to tell him everything was fine, but he didn't care about that. He said . . . he said . . ."

"He said what, Sally Ann?" Cynthia demanded, needing for her own sake to understand precisely what had happened here tonight, and why. Because if Tom had done this, if he had hit a woman, with or without provocation, it changed everything. How she felt about him, the outcome of the trial, his future relationship with Ryan, with her . . . it changed everything!

Sally Ann fought for control. "He started yelling at me about how he was never going to pay support money to me, or to Ryan! I tried to reason with him, to tell him that was just my lawyer's idea, not mine, but he wouldn't listen to anything I said."

Moving away from Cynthia, she took a deep, shaky breath and waved her arms bewilderedly in front of her. "Instead, he went on and on about how all I had ever wanted was his money and that I wasn't going to get it. Then...then—" she stared to sob again "—he demanded I hand Ryan over...and when I wouldn't—I didn't think he should be driving anywhere with Ryan when he was in such a state—he...he hit me!" She gingerly touched her jaw as new tears streamed down her face. Sobbing loudly and brokenly, she again buried her face in her hands.

Tom wouldn't have done that, Cynthia thought. He wouldn't have hit a woman, no matter what. He wouldn't have hit anyone. Even when that reporter had fallen into his yard, he hadn't hit him. But he'd wanted to, she remembered suddenly, as the picture of him with his fist drawn back, waiting, came into her mind. He'd almost hit him.

But then, that had been weeks ago, before everyone's emotions had worked up to a fever pitch, before the stress of the trial, before they'd made love....

He was a passionate man, strong-willed and determined. But he was also under a lot of stress. Was it possible he had been pushed over the edge? That Sally Ann had goaded him deliberately, egged on by her own sense of powerlessness in this situation?

But did that excuse his hitting her?

She thought not.

Cynthia gave a tortured sigh and closed her eyes, wondering when all this unpleasantness would ever end, and if it *would* ever end. She was so sorry she had agreed to get involved in this case. She was so tired of being in the middle.

"Where are Tom and Ryan now?" Cynthia asked in a trembling voice.

Sally Ann lifted her shoulders in a helpless shrug. "I don't know." She wiped the tears from her face. Her voice was muffled behind her hands as she tried to get a grip on herself. When she spoke again her voice was stern, hard, as if she were trying her best to be tough. "He didn't tell me where he was taking Ryan," she said. Two tears trailed down her cheeks and she brushed them away, and finished relating, in a weary unsettled voice devoid of all hope, "He just said something about being on to me, that my plan wasn't going to work, that I wasn't going to get any of his money. That if he had his way, I would never see Ryan again! Oh, Cynthia—" Sally Ann started to sob again without warning "—you don't think he's going to do anything crazy like try and run away with Ryan, do you?"

Run away! Now that was nonsense. "What are you talking about?" Cynthia demanded incredulously, her heart beginning to race even faster as the implications of what had just transpired set in. Tom had talked once about taking off with Ryan, fleeing the country, she remembered. But that had been just talk, hadn't it? Hadn't it?

"Sally Ann, calm down," she said firmly, thinking this all had to be one giant mistake. And yet how could she explain that bruise on Sally Ann's jaw or her near hysteria? How could she totally discount the rage Tom had been showing the past few days?

And he had stated to Judge Mitchum earlier he wanted no part of paying any child support to Sally Ann. He had been furiously unwilling about that, and rightly so, in her own estimation. But this...this was going too far. And she knew in her heart that Judge Mitchum would think so, too. That it wouldn't matter, really, if Sally Ann had provoked Tom. All that would matter was that he'd hit Sally Ann, and then fled—in open defiance of the court order—with his son. It was all Cynthia could do to suppress a moan of anguish.

"I can't calm down!" Sally Ann sobbed. "Don't you think I've tried?" She clutched at the policeman and held on to him for dear life, as if he were her last and only hope. "You've got to help me get my baby back, please! Oh please! I'm afraid Tom's going to do something terrible!"

Her mouth filled with the coppery taste of fear, Cynthia got hold of herself and went inside to use the phone. Yet even as she was walking, even as she thought of all the unpleasantness that had gone on in the courtroom the past few days, she couldn't believe any of this was really happening. This was a mistake, she told herself sternly. It was all some giant misunderstanding. Tom had a temper, yes, but he would never hit a woman, even if provoked. And he knew better than to simply run off with his own son against court's orders. He knew better. Tom wouldn't deliberately hurt anyone. And never in front of Ryan!

With numb, shaking fingers, she dialed Tom's number. Jasmine answered. When asked if she had seen Tom lately, she said casually, "Yes, he went to get Ryan a little while ago."

At that, Cynthia's heart plummeted. "But Ryan was visiting with Sally Ann at my house," she said in the most tranquil voice she could manage.

"Yes," Jasmine countered evenly, unperturbed, "and you got called away."

"How do you know that?" Cynthia asked, aware the policeman was at her elbow now, as was Sally Ann, both of them listening to her every word.

"Well, there was this messenger service looking for you. They called here first, trying to catch you, but you'd already left with Ryan to go over to your house. Tom waited a couple minutes, then phoned you, to make sure you'd gotten the message. And he, well, he found out from Sally Ann you had left her alone with Ryan. He wasn't very happy about that."

Neither was she at the moment. Nor would Judge Mitchum be when he heard.

Feeling as if her every limb was weighted down with a ton of marble, Cynthia tried to compose her thoughts, to make some sense of the nonsensical. But very little was gained from her frantic attempt to think, to formulate some defense for Tom, some reason for what he had apparently done. "Was he angry when he left?" she said finally, regaining a small modicum of her usual composure. This, too, was something the police would want to know. What was his state of mind when he left his house and headed toward Sally Ann?

There was a revealing silence on the other end of the phone. Finally Jasmine said reluctantly, "A little." There was a question in her voice that she was too smart to ask. Clearing her throat, she continued, more carefully now, "Anyway, he went over to pick up Ryan. He said if you weren't there to supervise, then Ryan couldn't be there, either. And that's the last I heard."

She spoke so matter-of-factly, Cynthia thought, as if nothing out of the ordinary had been going on.

"Why? What's happened?" Jasmine insisted.

Cynthia hesitated, thinking it would be better if the police talked to Jasmine and got her side of the story before she knew any other details. Finally she said, "It's too complicated to explain. Just do me a favor and ask Tom to stay there if he arrives. I...I have a few questions to ask him." So did the police, she knew.

Sally Ann confronted the officer as soon as Cynthia had hung up the phone. "You're not going to let him get away with this, are you?" she demanded. "The man beat me up!"

Just then, another squad car arrived. "We'll need you to press charges, if you want him picked up for assault," the first policeman said, getting out his pen and pad.

Sally Ann looked ready to do just that. "Fine," she said tightly. "Let's get on with it."

Surely, Cynthia thought in confusion, there had to be more to the story. Maybe there was a tussle, and maybe Sally Ann slipped and fell. But even as she thought it, the cold clinical side of her knew she was reaching for some mitigating circumstance that would let Tom off the hook. For the simple fact remained that Sally Ann had very definitely been slugged in the jaw. Ryan was gone. So was Tom. The evidence might only be circumstantial, but it was pretty damning.

Always before, she had been able to separate her personal and professional lives. But this time she couldn't. If Tom had done this, then she didn't know him at all.

She suddenly felt old and disillusioned, traumatized, too, as if she were the one who had sustained the shock of the confrontation and the beating, and not Sally Ann.

Had everything she thought she knew about Tom been a lie? Had she seen in him only what he wanted her to see? What she wanted to see? It hurt and saddened her to realize that because of his attractiveness, the chemistry between them, her own loneliness, that she might have allowed herself to be led down a primrose path.

Cynthia turned away from everyone wearily, composing herself with effort. She knew what she had to do.

While the first policeman stayed behind to take a statement from Sally Ann, the second policeman accompanied Cynthia to Tom's house.

Jasmine, looking puzzled, let them in. To Cynthia's further surprise, Tom was inside with Ryan acting as if nothing at all had happened, which was hardly the behavior of a normally law-abiding man who had just assaulted a woman, she thought. Maybe it hadn't happened as Sally Ann described, she thought on a burst of hope.

However, as she got close enough to see his face, she could tell that under his surface cool Tom seemed very angry, if controlled. Seeing the way he glared at her, as if she had just betrayed him in the most heinous of ways, her heart sank.

I have to be fair here. I have to let him tell his side of the story.

Cynthia held up a hand, before the policeman could speak. "Tom, what happened just now at my house?" she asked, hoping against reason he could somehow vindicate himself from this mess, from the violence. "Why did you bring Ryan home with you? You know he's supposed to be visiting with his mother." *Please,* she thought, *let him have a good reason for whatever it is he's done.*

"And you were supposed to be supervising the two of them," he returned evenly, glancing first at Ryan, who was playing quietly on the floor, and then back at her. "Why did you leave them alone, Cynthia? What could be more important to you than the well-being of my son?" Hurt and bewilderment echoed in his low voice.

I didn't think anything would happen, she thought. "That's not the point, Tom," she said, then sighed heavily, wishing she could keep her own pain at bay. "The visitation wasn't over yet. And right now, Sally Ann is hysterical."

"She says you beat her up," the policeman cut in bluntly.

"What?" Tom was incredulous. He turned to face the cop, all color draining from his face.

"She's got a huge welt on her jaw," Cynthia said.

Tom sent her a betrayed look, his incredulity fading in the light of her thinly veiled accusation. "Well, I sure didn't put it here," he said adamantly.

"Tell it to the judge," the policeman said, walking forward to read Tom his rights. He handcuffed his hands behind his back.

Though Tom looked at her for help, Cynthia felt powerless. "Tell me what really happened, Tom." She bit back her own futile tears. "I want to help you, but I have to know the truth."

"I told you the truth!" he stormed. "I went over to get Ryan. I brought him home. That's all there was to it!"

He was evading now, the same way he had evaded and glossed over his past when he'd initially met Sally Ann. He was telling the truth—but only enough to allow him to still feel comfortable.

Without warning, her knees felt weak and she felt sick inside. She tried to think, to make herself slow the pounding of her heart, lessen the roar in her ears. She tried to take a deep breath, but her chest felt constricted. "You didn't argue with Sally Ann?" Cynthia asked. She looked deep into his eyes, searching for the truth.

Tom shook his head incredulously. "No, she wanted me to take him home with me. She said she was nervous about being there alone with him."

Nervous about being alone with Ryan! That, Cynthia could not believe. Sally Ann was determined to get every minute of time with Ryan she had coming to her, and she'd been quite at ease when Cynthia had left. She loved Ryan, and Ryan loved her. "You didn't argue with her about the support money her lawyer asked for today in court?" Cynthia pressed.

"No." Tom's tone was hard, contentious as he went on, "Although, believe me, I would've liked to. I still have no intention of ever paying her a cent, and I think for them to even suggest I might do so shows incorrigible gall!"

The policeman made a faint grunting sound, as if what Tom had just said explained it all.

Tom's gaze narrowed. He looked at Cynthia as if expecting her to wave some magic wand and bail him out. He didn't understand why she didn't, and as the moments passed he seemed to become more and more bewildered. In a raspy voice, he asked, "What's going on here? Cynthia? Why are you letting them do this to me?"

Don't you understand that it's out of my control? she thought, perilously near tears. She didn't want any part of putting Tom in jail. She wanted only to help him, but she couldn't unless he told her the truth, unless he showed some remorse for what he'd done, and admit that this one time he may have gone too far in pulling out all the stops to achieve his goal.

She buried her face in her hands. She had warned Tom earlier he had to lighten up, take things more in stride, stop railing against fate. If only he had listened to her instead of trying to take his destiny into his own hands. Because in his quest not to do nothing and become a victim, he had instead become an aggressor who was about to go to jail.

The policeman went to use the phone, and when he returned he said, "My partner's taken Ms. Anderson to the hospital. He thinks she should have her jaw looked at."

Tom swore and shook his head in anger and confusion. "I don't believe this. I don't believe any of it!"

Afraid he was going to lose control completely, which would reflect badly on his case, Cynthia wanted to warn him to hold his formidable temper. She wanted to say something that would ease this awful tension between them and make everything better, but she didn't know quite what. Obviously there was more going on here than either party had told them. Whether or not they'd ever get to the whole truth, Cynthia didn't know.

She only knew it hurt her to see Tom standing there, his hands handcuffed behind his back like some common criminal. "Tom, I—"

Ignoring her, he said over his shoulder to Jasmine, "Call my lawyer. Have her meet me at the police station and bring money for bail. It looks like I'm going to need it."

He turned back to Cynthia, his hurt palpable in the strained silence. And then she knew. If she had taken a knife and stabbed it into his stomach, she couldn't have hurt him more.

Chapter Twelve

Cynthia was all business when she walked into the jail where Tom was being held. As it was policy to hold anyone arrested for assault for twenty-four hours minimum—what the courts considered a cooling-off period—he wouldn't be released until the evening. Meanwhile, Cynthia needed to talk to him.

Judge Mitchum was not at all happy about the latest turn of events. And the media, when they'd found out about it, had gone crazy. Tom's photo was on the front page of every newspaper in the city. Public sentiment was running strong against him now. And that could affect the outcome of the case—if it hadn't already been decided the moment he'd taken a swing at his son's mother.

The corrections officer led her back to a conference room. She was just putting her briefcase up on the table when Tom was escorted in the other door. In jail-issue denim shirt and pants, with his hair rumpled, his face unshaved, he looked tired and menacing. And still angry as all get out.

Swallowing hard, Cynthia sat down. The corrections officer positioned himself next to the door. As per jail policy, he would remain there throughout the duration of their interview.

Cynthia got out paper and pen and turned on her tape recorder. "I need your side of the story for my report to the court."

Tom gave her a steady, uncooperative look and his voice was flat and hard when he replied, "I gave that to you yesterday."

He had denied hitting Sally Ann. The bruise on her jaw said otherwise, and it looked even worse this morning than it had the previous day. Other evidence, as well, seemed to confirm Sally Ann's story.

"There were airline tickets to Montreal, made out in your name, yesterday afternoon. The flight was to have left at ten last night."

His brow furrowed. "I don't know what you're talking about."

"Tom, please," she whispered, forgetting for a moment her determination to keep this strictly professional. She switched off her recorder. "Don't lie to me. It won't do you any good. The only thing that could possibly help now is if you admit what happened and tell me what was going on in your mind yesterday. Stress can do strange things to people. I know that. I've had times myself where I've almost blown up, where something happens and it feels like the last straw, just too much to take, and I want to hit something or throw something." Her voice caught but she pushed on determinedly, knowing she had to get the truth from him now no matter how painful it was to either of them, "I know how much you love Ryan. I know how this whole thing has driven you crazy." Tears stung her eyes and she blinked them away. Huskily, she continued, "It wasn't right, what you did yesterday, but in light of all that has happened, it *is* understandable.''

His eyes, which had turned an almost obsidian blue, glared at her. His hands clenched into fists on the table between them. Her gaze was drawn to the coiled strength in them and she shivered involuntarily, thinking what it must be like to be on the wrong side of his formidable temper. ''For the last time,'' he ground out between clenched teeth, ''I did not hit Sally Ann! I did not assault her! I did not forcibly take Ryan from her!''

Steam was practically coming from his nostrils as he finished and sat back, his spine pressed flat against the back of the chair. The corrections officer moved forward slightly, checking to see if everything was okay. Cynthia nodded, and he stepped back against the door.

''You had no plans to take Ryan and fly to Montreal last night?'' They both knew that technically he could disappear for as long as he wanted. He could write anywhere. He could sell his work to publishers in other English-speaking countries. It could be years before the red tape was untangled enough to allow for extradition, if they could even get it.

''None whatsoever,'' Tom grated, his low words accompanied by a withering glare.

She wanted to believe him. The emotional side of her did. But the logical side of her told her otherwise, when she looked at the evidence and remembered his voicing the desire to take Ryan and run. She knew how afraid he was of losing Ryan, how devastated by just the possibility. She knew from the way he had reacted in taking Ryan to the emergency room for that rash that he was a fiercely protective father. And she knew, from his reaction in court, that he considered Sally Ann not just a threat to his happiness, but to Ryan's, also.

It was Sally Ann who had gone to the press with her story against court orders. It was Tom who had finally lashed out and hit Sally Ann.

Part of this was her fault, she knew. She never should have left Sally Ann alone with Ryan. She focused on him again and turned on her tape recorder. "The package sent to me yesterday at my office. The IRS did not send it to me."

"You're blaming me for that, too?" His sarcasm was unchecked. "You think I did it just to get you out of the house so I could snatch Ryan from Sally Ann? Come on!"

She glanced up at him, her pulse thrumming, and was reminded suddenly of his passionate lovemaking that one reckless but memorable time. "What other explanation is there?" she asked, pushing the thought away, fighting the dryness in her throat. "I saw how virulently you reacted to the idea of paying support money to Sally Ann—"

"At least you've got that straight!" he snapped. As if he found it painful to look into her eyes, his gaze drifted lower, to her mouth, and lower still, to her breasts, before returning to collide once again with her searching gaze.

"But Sally Ann told me she didn't want it."

His glance narrowed and he shook his head in disgust. His chair scraped the floor as he pushed back from the table. "If you believe that, you're more naive than I thought. Face it, we've both been duped, Cynthia, you most of all." He stood and growled to the guard, "Get me out of here."

"Tom . . ." Cynthia stood up, feeling helpless, tears filling her eyes. He turned to look at her. She saw a brief flash of regret, then a dismissive look. "If you had just let things go on," she pleaded, "the way they were, let them take their natural course," she warned sadly, "instead of taking matters into your own hands, it would have all worked out. Maybe not the way you wanted it, but . . ."

Contempt curled the edges of his mouth. He was finished trying to explain himself to her. He was sorry he'd ever tried. "Go write your report," he said in a silken tone that sent ominous shivers of warning up and down her spine. His glance narrowed even more. "Just remember, when you're in court, you're supposed to do what's best for Ryan."

He still felt that what was best for Ryan was him, Cynthia knew. And so had she—at one time. But now . . . now she didn't know. He was filled with rage, a rage she didn't see letting up soon. Oh, she knew firsthand what a gentle, caring, considerate man Tom could be. Nor could she forget how tender he had been with her, how giving. But she also knew how angry he could get. How physical. It was just a shame that this time, when he'd felt his temper flying out of control, he hadn't been on a tennis court to vent it harmlessly.

Not surprisingly, Cynthia was so hurt and depressed and upset by all that had gone on that she couldn't sleep that night, or the next, or the next, and by the time court resumed on Monday, she was a jittering bundle of nerves.

As she had expected, she was the last person called to testify for the plaintiff. Her knees were shaking as she approached the stand and was sworn in. She sat down, forcing herself to look at Sally Ann's attorney. "You've had ample time to observe Sally Ann with her son," he said. "Is she a loving, responsive mother?"

"Yes, very much so."

"The two have bonded well?"

"Very well, under the circumstances." Cynthia swallowed hard, trying to keep the nervousness out of her voice. It wasn't easy because she could feel Tom's gaze fixed on her, hard and contemptuous. She knew he felt betrayed, even though she was only telling the truth. She also knew she had no choice. Continuing to look at Myron Singleton, she said, "Ryan runs to his mother whenever she arrives. He kisses and hugs her freely, and that affection is returned."

"What about Mr. Harrigan?" Myron continued. "What kind of father is he?"

"He's also loving and patient, extremely caring and attentive." She smiled, thinking of all the times she had seen Tom hug Ryan and Ryan hug Tom back.

"What drawbacks does he have?"

Cynthia had known this was coming. Yet she had to take a deep breath before she could answer. "He has a temper." It hurt her to say the words, even though they were fact. She lowered her glance, wishing they didn't have to talk about what had happened the other day.

But of course they did, and to both Cynthia's and Tom's agony, his alleged assault and subsequent arrest were gone over in great detail. Tom was no longer looking at Cynthia, but had buried his face in his hands. "So, in light of all this, what is your recommendation as to Ryan's placement?" Judge Mitchum asked.

The moment of truth. Her hands began to shake and she had to clamp them together firmly. She swallowed, aware Tom was looking at her again, hope etched in every line of his face. And only a few days ago he'd had good reason to hope. But now...

"I recommend the child be placed with his mother," she said finally, her throat so parched it ached. All the light went out of Tom's face. It was all she could do to continue, "With liberal visitation rights accorded to his father."

It was the only way, she thought, until they could determine that his temper was under control. The only way. And yet he looked as if she had just taken a dagger and driven it right through his heart.

Just that quickly, Cynthia had an image of Tom in the future, waking alone, without Ryan to make breakfast for. She thought about how empty his home would be, how quiet and tomblike. How devoid of joy. If the judge accepted her recommendation, Tom would have Ryan for visits, but it wouldn't be the same; they both knew it. He was losing his son, and it was all because he hadn't had the patience to wait for things to settle down and work themselves out. *Oh, Tom,* she thought brokenly, *why, oh why did you have to try and take justice into your own hands? Why did you have to do this to yourself and to Ryan?*

"Thank you," Judge Mitchum said, "you may step down, Ms. Whittiker." Looking up at all those gathered in the courtroom, he said, "We'll take a fifteen-minute recess, and then court will resume with counsel for the defense."

Cynthia and Tom stepped out into the hallway. Jasmine pushed forward to her side. "How could you do that to Tom?'' she demanded. "I thought you were his friend!"

I am, Cynthia thought. *In fact, a few days ago I was much more than that.* But looking at Tom as he stared back at her bleakly, all the betrayal, the hurt he felt evident on his face, she couldn't help but think it was all over, forever. He turned on his heel and stalked away.

As she watched him go, Cynthia thought her heart would shatter. The sick feeling in her stomach increased and she felt for a moment, before she got hold of herself, that she might faint. Her legs shaking, she went to get a drink of water and sit down.

She thought she had braced herself for his wrath. But she had been wrong. There was no bracing herself for the loss, the desolation, she felt now. For without Tom, and without Ryan, what meaning did her life have?

She knew how he felt, and it killed her to have been the one to have to recommend against placing Ryan with Tom. But what choice had she had? The answer was none. None at all. Even if someone else had been Ryan's guardian, the recommendation would have been the same, if not harsher.

Fortunately for Tom, Cynthia realized with a sharp sense of relief just moments after court resumed, his lawyer had really done her job. She brought out character witness after character witness, including every member of his family, as well as his friends and neighbors. Without exception, the reports were all glowing and complimentary, solidly based on, and supported by, factual accounts of his goodness.

His editor, Toby Williams said, "Tom has his priorities in order. He could be raking in twice the royalties, if only he would consent to the kind of world tour, rife with publicity gimmicks, we'd like to send him on, but he isn't interested at all. His whole life revolves around Ryan. He couldn't care less about fame or fortune. All he wants is to make sure Ryan is safe and happy..."

Jasmine said, "He's been a really good friend to me and my husband, Frank, and a substitute father for my boys. Frankly he has more patience with them than I could ever manage." And she went on to talk about some of the scrapes the boys had gotten themselves into and how Tom had helped her deal with their mischief in her husband's absence.

Cynthia could tell Judge Mitchum and the others in the courtroom were impressed with the outpouring of love for Tom. Nonetheless, it was his own testimony about his son that made the lasting impression.

When asked why he'd engaged a surrogate, he told the court, "I've always wanted a family like the one I grew up in—warm and loving. I've always wanted to have a child of my own. But it didn't happen that way for me, and so I began looking for alternate ways to have a family. I knew I could adopt, but I really wanted a child of my own flesh and blood, a part of me. If I'd known then what would happen—" His voice broke off abruptly. His regret and frustration, his fear, were almost a tangible presence in the room.

His eyes fell on Cynthia, and she knew that the grim reality of this hearing had finally sunk in for him, that there was no more pretending he could somehow do something that would make everything right, that would take both himself and his beloved son magically out of jeopardy. There were forces in action against him now, which he was powerless to fight. It no longer mattered what he wanted or felt was right. His destiny's and Ryan's were out of his hands, and he was shaken to the core of his being.

A part of him still had trouble accepting the fact she had advised placing Ryan with his mother. The betrayal he felt over what she'd said while on the stand was deep and lancing, and something he might not be able to overlook—ever—even if his exemplary behavior for most of the past won out over his recent loss of his temper and he was awarded custody of Ryan.

Cynthia clenched her teeth and crossed her arms at her waist. She had done the right thing in telling the truth. Now all they could do was wait and hope for an outcome that was just and fair.

Maybe... maybe this would somehow work out, after all, she prayed.

Aware Tom was still looking at her, almost begging her for help now, almost begging her to retract what she'd said earlier, she lowered her glance.

"Tell us how you feel about your son," his lawyer continued.

Tom turned his attention back to the court, and after a moment he continued in a voice that was slightly calmer, "When Ryan was born," he said softly, honestly, "I thought that all my dreams had come true. That I finally had what I'd been yearning for, that my life was complete." There was another pause. He seemed suddenly to be fighting the urge to break down and cry, and when he continued his voice was hoarse. "Even when he's cranky and trying my patience to the absolute limit—which I'll be the first to admit he sometimes does—I still love him." He blinked and went on even more hoarsely, "All I want is for him to remain in the same safe, secure environment he's known since I brought him home from the hospital over a year ago."

With a breaking voice he finished, "I love Ryan with all my heart. I've been a good father to him in the past and I'll be a good father to him in the future."

His attorney rested her case. Then Myron Singleton brought up the assault charge and tried to make it stick, while Tom flatly denied ever laying so much as a finger on Sally Ann. And then it was over. The lawyers made their final pitches, and everyone went home to wait.

The judge, feeling this had dragged on long enough, made his decision over the weekend. On Monday morning Tom, his family and friends, Sally Ann with some of her friends, their lawyers, the court officials, and Cynthia were seated and waiting tensely in the courtroom.

"I don't have to tell you all what a difficult case this has been," Judge Mitchum began, lowering his horn-rimmed glasses to the bridge of his nose. "The ultimate issue here is not what is best for the adults, but what is best for the child. In light of the recent assault charge against Mr. Harrigan, the court feels it is in Ryan's best interest to be placed with his mother, Sally Ann Anderson, for the time being...."

Placed with his mother.

The words echoed over and over in her head. Cynthia felt so numb and sick she could hardly speak, and then it was over, Sally Ann was leaping up joyously to hug her attorney. But Cynthia had eyes only for Tom. He looked as if his whole world had come to an end.

And if it had, Cynthia thought dismally, there was no chance at all that he'd ever be able to forgive her.

It didn't matter that she cared about him, or that he had once cared about her. All that mattered was Ryan was gone, his son was gone, and Cynthia was the person who more than anyone else had helped take him away.

WASN'T IT FUNNY, Tom thought, aware he was treading on the edge of hysteria. He still couldn't believe this was really happening. Any of it. One minute he and Ryan had been happy, the next in jeopardy. Now they weren't to be anything at all except another child separated from his father.

His vision blurred with tears, and he determinedly blinked them away. There would be plenty of time later, after Ryan had gone, to indulge himself in his grief.

He picked up Ryan's shirts and shorts, the rompers he had recently been learning to unsnap himself. Ryan's blankets and crib sheets were already loaded into the car. He wanted Ryan to have as many familiar things around him as possible. Bad enough Tom wasn't going to be there now.

"Are you doing all right, Tom?" His sister, Linda, came into the nursery. Her blue eyes were awash with tears, and it was all he could do not to break down and sob. He nodded. "I keep thinking this is some kind of bad dream, you know? Like I'm going to wake up and it's going to be all over." He gritted his teeth and inhaled deeply to ease the unbearable tightness in his chest.

"I know." The tears Linda had been holding back fell in rivulets down her cheeks. She hugged him hard and was barely able to let go. "But you can't lose hope. You heard what your lawyer said, Tom. As soon as they clear you on this assault charge, you can appeal."

Tom wished that possibility were a viable one. "Fat chance of that," he said bitterly. Everyone—including Cynthia, the one person he had figured would never believe that pack of lies—had assumed he had struck Sally Ann because he'd been provoked. Oh, his family insisted he was innocent, too. But he knew that deep in their hearts they all questioned whether or not he had done it; without exception, all felt he had been provoked by Sally Ann's lawyer's request for support payments, on top of everything else, although none of them condoned physical violence. Not for any reason.

Ryan toddled over to Mike and wrapped both his arms around Tom's legs. "Boo!" he said, grinning.

Tom pretended to have been greatly scared. "Boo!" he said back. Ryan giggled wildly, and just the sound of his laughter made Tom want to sob. He bent down to take his son into his arms.

His brother Mike and his parents walked into the room. "Let's take all this out to the car for him," Mike said with excessive gruffness, clearly in as much pain as Tom. Tom looked at him gratefully; that was one chore he couldn't bear to do. Goodbyes had always been tough for him, but this . . . this was unreal. The hurt was unreal.

"I think Tom and Ryan need a moment or two alone," his mother said gently. One by one everyone exited.

The nursery was stripped almost bare.

The door shut behind them and Tom sat down in the rocking chair. Ryan lifted a finger and touched it to his father's face, feeling the wetness. He gave Tom a quizzical look, and tears started in his eyes, too, in a natural empathy. Tom knew he'd better say goodbye before he broke down completely.

"I wish I had the words to explain all this to you, big guy, but I can't say as I understand it that much myself," he began hoarsely, struggling to control his voice. He took a deep breath, trying for Ryan's sake to sound positive. "You're going to go and live with your mama for a while now. I'll still visit you two times a week. I'm allowed to bring you back here every other weekend. So it's not like we're going to be apart for too long. And when you get a little older, well, heck, you can call me on the phone and talk to me everyday, let me know how you're doing." He had to grit his teeth to keep from crying, but after a couple of moments the intense concentration worked.

In the interim, he gently rubbed his son's back in soothing circular motions. He was glad to see Ryan's tears disappear, as his own had. It was important to help his son get through this, Tom knew. The pain would come later, in great numbing blows he would be powerless to circumvent.

I wish you didn't have to go, Tom thought. *I wish I didn't have to let you go.*

But he did, for now anyway. Until the time when he could get the court's decision overturned.

"Tom?" His mother knocked and stuck her head in. "Cynthia Whittiker is here. She said it's almost time."

Tom nodded, his grasp on his son tightening protectively.

Cynthia.

He'd expected her name to bring on an onslaught of anger, but it didn't. Not today. Today, it didn't bring up anything. Not hate. Not love. Nothing. Maybe he was too numb now to feel. He wondered if he would always be numb where she was concerned, or if one day he would be able to feel something for her again.

He stood, aware his legs had gotten shaky, and started for the door.

I can't do it, he thought, stopping. The urge to bolt and run was very strong. But he also knew he couldn't put Ryan through a life on the run. *I have to do as Judge Mitchum ordered, I have no choice,* he thought, but still he couldn't move, couldn't make himself take one more step toward letting Ryan go.

And then Cynthia was there, lifting Ryan from his arms. He stopped her before she could walk away, a light hand on her arm as he noted Ryan already had an arm wrapped around her neck. Ryan's other hand was tightly clutching an edge of Tom's shirt.

He didn't want to let go, either, Tom thought.

He leaned forward and pressed a kiss on the soft, baby-scented hair. "Goodbye, Ryan. I love you," he said, his voice catching. "And I'll see you in a couple of days."

Before he'd even drawn back all the way, Ryan seemed to understand what was happening. "Daddy!" he cried. "Daddy!" His anguished screams filled the air, more poignant and enraged than after any vaccination at the doctor's office.

"Dammit, Tom," Tom's father said, "if you'd just done what we advised and compromised in the beginning, you'd at least have him half the time."

"Tom, don't," Rachel admonished her husband. "That's in the past now. We have to go forward."

Go forward, Tom thought sadly. To what?

Meanwhile Ryan continued to wail. Tears in her own eyes, Cynthia had all she could do to hold on to him.

Tom was embroiled in a pain unlike any he'd ever felt, and beside him, his mother collapsed weeping into his father's arms. It was Linda who stepped forward to extricate Ryan's fingers, and who tried her best to soothe him as Cynthia hurried him from the room. Mike stepped in front of Tom, barring his move to interfere. "You don't want to do that, big brother," he said, his own eyes shimmering with emotion. "I know how you feel, believe me, but you've got to think things through now. Go through the courts. You don't want to end up in jail because then you'd still lose Ryan. At least this way, hard as it is, you'll be able to see him, do him some good."

Some good.

The phrase was so pitifully inept Tom shut his eyes.

And then his brother's wife, Diana, was beside him, pressing a glass of whiskey in his hands. "Here, Tom, drink this. It'll help. Trust me."

At that moment, Tom would have done anything to kill the pain. The only problem was, as he soon discovered, nothing, absolutely nothing, worked.

"Tom?" The house was dark as Cynthia peered in the front window. Gone were all the cars from the Harrigan entourage. Only Tom's remained in the drive.

She knew he was here. The front windows were open, the gentle spring breeze gently wafting in and out. So was the front door, she discovered several seconds later.

She pushed it open, switching on the entry light as she walked inside. "Tom?" she called louder.

Again, no answer.

Her heart pounding, not knowing what she would find, she moved hurriedly into the living room. He was on the sofa, feet propped up on the coffee table. There was a whiskey bottle on the table. Several ounces were missing, and an empty tumbler was in his hand. Tom was staring sightlessly at the fireplace in front of him.

"I just wanted you to know that Ryan is fine," Cynthia said around the lump of emotion in her throat. She continued on a breath of despair, "He settled down the moment we reached Sally Ann's place. She's taken the next couple of weeks off, so there'll be no problem there. And Tom, she's even thinking about bringing Ryan here—to you—during the day while she works."

The offer from Ryan's mother had been unstintingly generous under the circumstances. Cynthia was glad to find her so willing to try to work things out, apparently thinking the more Ryan saw of both parents the better, but it had puzzled her, too. She had expected Sally Ann to harbor too much bitterness after the assault.

For a long moment, Tom didn't budge. Finally he sighed and sat up straighter, bringing his feet down onto the floor. The action was mild and restrained, but beneath the surface was a depression so great it seemed insurmountable. He shoved his empty glass on the coffee table. "That's great," he said in a monotone. And then somewhat acerbically, "How very generous of her."

His voice was slurred, bitter, hurt.

Knowing she'd had a hand in his hurt sent a mist of tears to her eyes. She looked at him through her helplessness and pain. "I'm surprised your family left."

He shrugged, as if it no longer mattered, as if nothing mattered. "My dad's still ticked off at me. He told me all along this was going to happen and I wouldn't listen to him." He sighed heavily. "I'm not in the mood for any more I-told-you-so's from them or any pep talks from Mike or Linda. Anyway, I told them I wanted to be alone." His voice was gruff, hoarse, defiant.

Cynthia nodded. She was truly worried about him. She didn't know what she had expected of him now, but not this heavy, all-consuming sadness. He'd always been such a fighter, ever since she'd first known him. She had never expected him just to give up, but that was apparently what he was doing. The unfairness of it all scorched her soul. She wanted to help but just didn't know how, and that made her even angrier—not at anyone in particular, but at the world in general.

There was so much to say, and absolutely nothing, save Ryan, that would ease the pain. "Tom, I'm sorry," she said finally.

He focused on her, his blue eyes brilliant with suppressed wrath. "Are you really?"

She knew he needed to vent some of the anger he was feeling; she wasn't so sure she wanted to be the target. She hadn't done this to him; he'd done it to himself by assaulting Sally Ann. As much as she still didn't want to believe that, the facts said otherwise. "Yes," she said quietly with conviction. "I am sorry. I never wanted you to be hurt."

"But I am hurt." He picked up the whiskey bottle and slowly capped it. He picked up the glass and walked out to the spotless kitchen. He set the glass slowly in the sink, then turned to face her. The house seemed so silent, so achingly empty. "I think you'd better go." His voice was husky and tired, defeated. He looked in many ways like he would never recover from this loss.

She wanted to help, but knew there was no way in hell he was going to let her. No way he'd let anyone, in the mood he was in.

She saw he needed his space. "All right," she said finally, her trembling lower lip the only indication of the thousand and one emotions she was feeling, "I'll go, but if you need anything or... or want to talk—"

His answer was a harsh, grating laugh. "Yeah, I've seen the way you're here for me, Cynthia. I've seen the way you believe in me. Next thing I know you'll be telling me that given time everything will work out on its own...." His words were laced with biting sarcasm.

She winced. "As a matter of fact," she said, "I was going to say just that."

"Yeah, well, don't bother." He turned and, both hands cupping the edge of the sink, looked out over the backyard. "I had my chance to take destiny in my own hands, to take Ryan and run away before any of this ever even got to court, and I didn't do it. So in that sense—" he turned back to her, complacent now, self-indicting, remorseful ''—I have no one to blame but myself for what's happened.''

She stared at him incredulously. ''How can you say that?'' she countered, appalled he was still holding on to his he-man view of the world. ''It was your own temper that cinched this case against you. That and your refusal to compromise, to accept split custody as a workable alternative.'' One Sally Ann was more or less proposing even now with her offer to let Tom baby-sit Ryan while she worked.

At her harsh words, his eyes darkened unpleasantly. His frown deepening, he took a deliberate step toward her, as if trying to frighten her, to intimidate her physically so that she would get the blazes out of there and leave him in peace.

The cowardly part of her wanted only to comply; the woman who had come to love him with all her heart knew she had to stay, had to help bring about some change in him for Ryan's sake, as well as his own. So, she defiantly held her ground, sure on some level that he wouldn't hurt her. He might not like what she had to say, but he was going to hear it, anyway, because like it or not there were some things about him that had to change if he was ever going to get along in this world, and foremost among them was his refusal to accept that sometimes life and Tom Harrigan were going to be less than perfect. And that less than perfect didn't mean one had to give up!

''You're wrong, Cynthia. It wasn't my temper that clinched this,'' he corrected with venom, remaining precisely in place. ''Sally Ann's lies cinched the case against me. But I don't suppose you or anyone else will ever believe that, and since I've no way to prove it . . ." He turned away in frustration.

The silence between them was strained and heavy with an exasperation that was mutual and all-inclusive. And beyond that was a sadness for the romance between them that was never going to be.

A wave of defeat and anguish washed over her. She wondered numbly how she had ever thought that they would be able to get past this, go on to recover and to forgive, put the pieces of their shattered lives back together. But he was never going to be able to forgive her, and even if he could forgive, he wouldn't be able to forget. He knew it as well as she.

His hand came up to touch her face. "I did love you, you know," he said softly, sadly. "That's why I kissed you that night in Galveston, why I came to see you later, why I stayed and made love to you. Because I loved you. I just didn't know how or if I should say it then."

Tears blurred her eyes as she absorbed the words she had subconsciously yearned to hear for weeks now. "I know," she whispered back, her heart throbbing with a slow heavy funereal cadence. She tasted the salt of her tears on her lips. "I loved you, too." *I still do,* her heart cried. But it was too late. It had been from the moment she testified against him.

Slowly his hand dropped and he stepped back. He shook his head at her remonstratively, as if the matter were already closed and any arguments on her part would not only be futile, but painful. And pain was something he'd had more than enough of lately. "I've got to get to work," he said, running a hand through his hair.

"Now?" She wanted him to ask her to stay, to let her be with him, to help him.

He wanted none of that. His eyes were bleak, implacable. "Trust me. At the moment, it's the best thing—the only thing—I can do." He started to say more, then stopped, deciding now was not the time. And she wondered then if there would ever be another chance for the two of them. Right now, she wouldn't lay odds on it.

"You know the way out," he said softly, ignoring her disappointed, heartbroken look.

His lips pressed together firmly, he turned and walked away from her. His office door shut behind him. And the sound of that wood hitting wood had a finality to it that pierced her soul.

Chapter Thirteen

"Of course I'm happy about the court's decision," Sally Ann told an enthralled television audience later that same week. "I see it as a positive step not just for myself and my baby but for all women. Because if there's one thing I've learned over the past few months," she said, her face softening maternally, "it's that there really is a very special bond between a mother and a child. It's a bond that is instinctive, primal." She paused, reflecting back. "It certainly hit me when I least expected it."

At the interviewer's prodding, Sally Ann went on to talk about her recent involvement in an organization called Women Against Surrogacy. She now felt all surrogacy was wrong, and should be outlawed in every state in the country.

Having witnessed the heartbreak in the Harrigan case, Cynthia had to agree. No woman should rent out the use of her body, and her ova, for a fee.

So in a way she understood Sally Ann's using the opportunity given her to warn other people not to enter into surrogacy contracts. Sally Ann had always been a person who gave unselfishly of herself and was devoted to helping others—in her nursing career, and in her personal life. It was only natural she would want to save others from heartbreak if she could.

But there was Ryan to be considered, too, Cynthia thought, perturbed. Sally Ann had been spending an awful lot of time lately talking to reporters from newspapers and magazines. There was even talk of her going on a national TV news show.

Needing to be sure, for her own sake, that she had done the right thing in recommending Sally Ann have custody, Cynthia dropped by to see her the following afternoon.

"You're getting ready to move?" she remarked, as she walked in. Boxes were everywhere.

"Yes, I found a perfect little house to rent near the hospital. It has a fenced backyard with lots of trees, room for a swing and sandbox out back, and a sidewalk out front."

"It sounds lovely," Cynthia said.

"It is." Sally Ann smiled in contentment.

"How's Ryan?" Cynthia asked. As she spoke, a sleepy murmur came from the other room.

"Well, I was going to say he was napping, but—" Sally Ann grinned "—I hear he's awake. Hang on, and I'll go get him."

She disappeared into the bedroom down the hall and returned a moment later, Ryan in her arms. His features were still flushed with a sleepy look as he nestled contentedly in his mother's arms. He yawned and nestled closer still. Cynthia thought there had never been a more perfect picture of mother and child. Maybe she had been wrong to worry. Maybe these nagging feelings that something was amiss were just reaction to the custody outcome.

Thusly reassured, she was about to go when Sally Ann asked her to stay. "Please, we haven't really had a chance to talk, and so much has happened! I want to tell you all about it. I can put some coffee on, and Ryan can have some juice. It'll be just like old times, kind of."

Cynthia was curious to know in detail how they were adjusting. "Okay. Thanks."

Moments later, they were ensconced in the kitchen. Ryan was sitting in his high chair, contentedly munching on dry Cheerios and sipping apple juice from a two-handled drinking cup with a tight-fitting plastic lid. The two women were sitting at the table, coffee cups and plates of homemade carrot cake in front of them.

"How are things with you and Tom?" Cynthia asked. Since she had last seen him she hadn't ventured over there again. She'd sensed he needed time alone, time to accept everything that had happened. Only then could they see about repairing their relationship, and although it hurt to stay away she knew right now it was for the best.

Sally Ann was silent a long moment. Then, "I dropped the assault charge against him."

Cynthia was stunned; she hadn't heard. "Why?" she said. Before Sally Ann had been so determined to press charges.

She shrugged and stared into her cup. "It didn't seem right—him being Ryan's father and all—and I didn't want the hassle of going to court again. I just wanted to put it behind me." She looked up and took a deep breath. "Get on with my life, you know?"

"What did Tom say?"

"I don't know. We haven't talked about it." Again she looked away.

Cynthia sensed there was more going on here than Sally Ann wanted her to know. "How are the two of you getting along otherwise?" she asked gently.

Sally Ann's eyes filled. "Well, I'd like to say he's forgiven me completely for reneging on my half of the surrogacy contract, but—" her mouth quivered slightly "—that would be stretching it." She wiped the corners of her eyes with her index finger. "He's been civil, though, and I've been trying to do my part to end this animosity between us by letting him see Ryan every day. I think he appreciates that." Her mouth quivered again as she related shakily, "In fact, he had him all morning today while I was here packing."

"That was nice of you," Cynthia said softly. She knew what an emotional issue this was, how hard it was for Tom and Sally Ann to discuss. She also knew how much Tom must miss Ryan; Sally Ann's generosity would help him make the transition with less difficulty and heartache.

"We've even talked about Tom baby-sitting Ryan when I've used up all my vacation and go back to work the week after next. He's amenable to the idea, and I admit it would save me a lot of worry knowing that Ryan was well cared for in my absence." She was silent, looking faintly troubled again. "Neither of us really wants to put Ryan in a day-care center at this stage of his life if we can help it. We both want to give him as much one-on-one time and attention as possible."

Cynthia agreed that was best, but again she had the nagging feeling that something was wrong here. Part of it was the quick way Sally Ann had forgiven Tom all the bad blood that had gone on during the hearings. Of course, having won the dispute, Sally Ann was in a position to be generous, Cynthia thought. But would a woman really react that way to a person who'd assaulted her? She didn't think so.

Without warning, Tom's words came to mind. "It wasn't my temper that clinched this," he'd said. "Sally Ann's lies clinched the case against me."

She frowned again. Something about this just didn't figure, and try as she might, she couldn't rid herself of the unsettling feeling she was missing something. But it wasn't until she was leaving, though, that she saw further proof something was a little off.

In a dusty carton next to the door was an open box of books. Inside, were old copies of Tom's paperbacks and the hardcover book, *Crossbones and Terror*, that had made the *New York Times* bestseller list several years before. Although Tom had written the book under his pen name, his photo was on the back.

Just that swiftly, Sally Ann's testimony came to mind: "I didn't know who he was, just that he was a writer," Sally Ann had said.

But apparently she had known who he was all along, Cynthia thought, and had lied about it! What else had she lied about? Cynthia took a deep breath and felt her hands and knees tremble. She had made a terrible mistake before, believing everything Sally Ann had said, not believing Tom. She only hoped it wasn't too late to rectify it.

Turning, she saw that Sally Ann had just put Ryan in his playpen on the other side of the room, and he was now contentedly playing with his toys. The moment she looked at Cynthia's face she knew something was wrong.

Cynthia didn't mince words. "You knew who Tom was all along," she said slowly, her anger mounting. She'd been duped. And all this time, she'd thought Tom was the one who wouldn't own up to the truth. How far off the mark she'd been!

"I don't know what you're talking about," Sally Ann said, her face paling until the freckles stood out in dark brown blotches.

"Tom's books…" Cynthia pointed to the open box.

"I just bought them."

"The pages are yellowed, Sally Ann."

"At a used-book store."

Was she telling the truth? Cynthia walked over to the box, and picked up one of the books. On the back was a stick-on computer label. Cynthia stared at it, thinking quickly. Sally Ann had bluffed her way out of trouble before. She wasn't the only who could bluff. Cynthia began peeling off the label.

"What are you doing?" Sally Ann asked nervously.

"I'm going to take this label with me. I hope you don't mind."

"N-no. Why would I mind?" Sally Ann's chin lifted. "I just don't see why you'd want it."

"Simple. I'm going to take it back to the book store, and let them run this number through their files. You see, all the sales are computerized now. They can look at the numbers on the label, input them into the computer, and get all kinds of information spit back out at

them. What store it was sold at, the date, if the trans-
action was done by credit card or check—in which case
we'll have a name. It'll be easy for us to prove that you
weren't the one who bought this book new."

Sally Ann turned even whiter, and then very red.

"Of course if you can supply me with the name of
the used-book store and the date you bought these
books," Cynthia said, picking up another, "then none
of this will be necessary, but if not..." She let her voice
trail off.

Sally Ann swallowed again, hard. "I don't remember where the store is."

"Come on, Sally Ann. You said on the witness stand
that you didn't read very much except professional
publications and magazines. If you go to book stores
so infrequently, surely you would remember where and
when you made the purchase, particularly since it was
done so recently."

Sally Ann wet her lips and looked desperate. "Why
are you bugging me about this?"

"Because I think you lied," Cynthia said sternly,
"and I'm going to prove it. And once I do, I'll person-
ally ask Judge Mitchum to haul you into court for
perjury. And once that's done, how long do you think
this custody decision is going to last?"

Finally she'd struck a chord. "All right, all right,"
Sally Ann said in a low, distressed voice. "So I knew
all along Tom was the author of those books! So
what!" She sat down on a carton wearily, her hands
clasped loosely in front of her. She lifted her eyes to
Cynthia, seeming to beg for mercy. "I never asked to
be paired up with someone like Tom at the agency. It
just happened. Then once it did I kept waiting for him

to tell me who he was," she whispered. "How important a person he was, but he never did. After a while I figured he didn't want me to know. A lot of famous people are like that. They like to keep a low profile. We see it at the hospital all the time. Sure, there are local celebrities who want to hold press conferences before they leave the hospital, even if they've only been in for a routine appendectomy, but there are more of them who want to check in and out in complete anonymity. So I just figured I'd go along with him."

"But you lied about it on the stand!" Cynthia said aghast. "While you were under oath."

Sally Ann turned even redder. Fidgeting nervously, she stood up and completely avoided Cynthia's gaze. And suddenly, perhaps because of the guilty way she was acting, Cynthia knew that wasn't all the woman had lied about.

Thinking quickly, she went back over the case. Everything had gone more or less as expected—until the assault charge. Although all the evidence pointed to Tom's guilt, and the police had thought he was guilty, the idea of his hitting a woman had never seemed quite believable to her.

Tom was capable of great anger, yes, but she had never known him to hit anyone. Yes, he'd been rough with a trespassing reporter once, but he had never actually hit anyone.

Furthermore, when she had seen Tom that afternoon at his home on the afternoon of the alleged assault, he and Ryan had both been calm, acting as if nothing out of the ordinary had happened. Only Sally Ann had been sobbing hysterically, her face hidden in her hands. Surely a fight of the nature Sally Ann had described would have upset Ryan, and at least left Tom disheveled. But he hadn't been disheveled, and Ryan had been his usual happy little self.

And most important of all, wouldn't Sally Ann still be afraid of Tom, at least harbor some misgivings about how he might behave when he was alone with her? Instead she seemed to trust him completely. And why not, Cynthia thought angrily, if she had faked the assault as a last-ditch way to win the case? In fact, she'd probably gotten the idea from that picture on the *National Tattletale*—the one of Tom roughly pushing a reporter out of his yard.

"Well, at least I understand now why you dropped the assault charges against Tom."

"I—"

"You dropped them because the assault never happened, did it, Sally Ann? Did it?"

Sally Ann's throat worked and her eyes filled with tears.

"Who really hit you that day?" she asked with the intimidating fire she used when cross-examining a witness on the stand. "Did someone else help you? Or did you do it to yourself, after Tom left with Ryan—as you had asked him to do because you weren't feeling well?"

Sally Ann turned even redder. Realizing it would be futile at this point to lie, she merely shook her head and said brokenly, "You don't understand."

"Then explain it to me," Cynthia said harshly, furious she had allowed herself to be duped. "Explain to me why you made reservations to Montreal, Canada, for Tom and Ryan. Why you went to such lengths to discredit him."

"Because you favored him!" she shouted. "What do you think? That I'm an idiot? I saw the way you were falling in love with him, and I knew...I knew when it came time to say who Ryan should be with that you were going to pick Tom!"

"So you set out to put the odds in your favor, by lying and sending Tom to jail?" Cynthia said, aghast. When Sally Ann said nothing in response, she said, "How could you do that to him?"

"I didn't have any choice! Don't you see that?" Sally Ann sobbed. "I had to do it. I had to do it because I loved Ryan and I wanted him with me!" Her breath caught. "And I knew unless they turned up something bad about Tom that he was going to win."

"And the support money? You planned that, too, all along?"

She shook her head miserably. "No, that was my lawyer's idea. I didn't want a penny of it, but he felt I should have it—for Ryan's sake. I didn't know he was going to ask for it that day in court, but he did, and when I saw the look on Tom's face—and the look on everyone else's faces in that courtroom—I knew they all thought I was a terrible person, just out for Tom's money, that I had lost the case just that quickly, that my only chance was if Tom did something bad, too. Something even worse," she said on another wrenching sob.

"But you knew he wouldn't."

Sally Ann shook her head and wiped away her tears with the backs of her hands. "No, it didn't seem likely. I mean, I knew from the way he acted as soon as he left the courtroom that day that he had a bad temper. I think everybody must have heard him say he wouldn't pay child support to me, no matter what, the moment court was adjourned." She composed herself slightly. "And I saw for myself how angry he was that day. I was afraid for a minute that he just might hit me."

"But he didn't hit you, Sally Ann," Cynthia reminded her patiently.

"No, and I knew then he probably never would." Sally Ann's shoulders were hunched forward despairingly. "So I...I made his mistake for him."

"What do you mean?" Cynthia pressed.

Sally Ann's thin shoulders lifted and fell.

"You staged the whole thing. You hit yourself."

"All right, all right!" Sally Ann shouted. "I staged the assault!"

"How?" Silence. "I'm going to find out the whole truth, Sally Ann, so you might as well tell me everything."

Sally Ann was silent for a moment. Finally, in a low sullen voice, she began to talk. "I instructed the messenger service to call his place first and ask for you, then if you weren't there, as I knew you wouldn't be at that time of day, to call your place. I knew Tom would wonder about it and call you, that he would worry you'd leave me alone with Ryan. When he did, I told him I wasn't feeling well, and he came over to get Ryan early. After he left, I...I hit myself in the jaw with one of your heavy law books."

"And that made the bruise?"

She nodded.

Cynthia shook her head in disgust.

Sally Ann defended herself in a broken whisper. "I know it sounds crazy and maybe it was, but you have to understand I was just so desperate. I'd lost Ryan once and I couldn't bear the thought of that happening again, and I knew from the looks I saw on everyone's faces in that courtroom that it was about to happen again, that everyone was against me, that they thought I was a fool for ever agreeing to the surrogate contract in the first place.''

She sighed heavily, and her eyes filled with tears. She looked lost and forlorn and very, very tired. As if the burdens of the past months, the strain, were more than she could bear.

"And maybe I was," Sally Ann said softly, honestly. She threw up her hands in profound confusion. "I just don't know anymore," she whispered. "I can't regret letting Tom hire me to carry his baby because that's how I got Ryan. And yet if I had known about the pain it was going to cause all of us, I don't know if I would've gone through with it, but I know no one else ever should," she finished on a note of heartfelt conviction.

She had been far too desperate, Cynthia agreed. Was it possible Sally Ann had suffered a nervous breakdown the past few months? She'd had a lot to contend with: her illness, her sterility, seeing Ryan, the battle for custody.

Cynthia knew, from all the time she had spent with Sally Ann, that there was much good in her, too. Certainly Ryan loved her and was beginning to count on her. She was a good nurse and a kind person. She'd just let her desire to win custody of her son get out of hand.

Cynthia sighed, feeling very tired herself now. "I've got to tell Judge Mitchum everything I know," Cynthia said, after she'd taken a moment to absorb it all. And then she would have to tell Tom. What would he say? she wondered. What would he feel toward her, toward Sally Ann, now that the truth was out?

More tears poured from Sally Ann's eyes. She buried her face in her hands and sobbed with remorse, saying over and over again how sorry she was, how bad she felt.

Cynthia knew the pain she was hearing now was real, and that the ramifications of what Sally Ann had done weren't over yet, not by a long shot, and they wouldn't be until she saw Tom. And told him what she knew now.

"HOW'S WORK ON YOUR BOOK coming, son?" Tom Sr. asked, his comforting voice reverberating over the long-distance phone lines.

Tom stretched and leaned back in his office chair. He pushed the save button on the computer. "Your timing is excellent as usual, Dad. I just finished the first draft."

His dad hesitated. "You've gotten a lot done this week then?"

"It's kept me busy," Tom answered absently. The truth was he'd had to do something to stop thinking about Ryan, and the book had been the perfect outlet. He'd been able to pour all his emotional energy into finishing the manuscript. The demanding work had helped; the cathartic action leaving him drained yet satisfied on a professional level, if still somewhat depressed on a personal level. But even that was beginning to work itself out, he noted with faint pride. Which just went to prove, he figured, that Cynthia was right in her theory that a person could adjust to just about anything, given time.

"How are you holding up otherwise?" Tom Sr. asked gently.

"I'm doing okay," Tom said slowly.

"Tom, I've been thinking," his dad began with difficulty. "I, uh, well, I shouldn't have said some of the things I did."

"Why?" Tom cut in bluntly. He wanted to get everything out in the open. "You and Mom were right."

"Yes, but we didn't want to be."

"Well, it's all water under the bridge now," Tom said. He didn't want to waste anymore time being angry with them, or having them angry at him.

His father paused. "You're sure?"

Tom felt his eyes moisten unexpectedly; something that was happening to him a lot these days. But maybe that was to be expected, too. "I'm sure, Dad."

There was another silence, this one slightly less strained. "So, how is Ryan doing with Sally Ann?" Tom Sr. asked.

"Okay. Great, actually," Tom admitted, unable to completely mask his own surprise at that. He'd been so sure he was the only person who could adequately care for Ryan. "He seems very content, very happy—both with his mother and me. And Sally Ann's been generous, letting me see him every day for at least a few hours." Probably, he thought, because she felt guilty. But he wasn't going to quarrel with his good fortune.

Nor would he rail against fate any longer.

He was beginning to think that Cynthia had been right, that everything did work out in the long run, given time, and that some things were just meant to be, that one way or another they would all end up where they were meant to be. For Ryan, it had been to have two parents who loved him, both a large part of his life.

For Sally Ann—although she hadn't known it at first—Ryan had been her last chance to bear a child. The child of her own that she had always wanted, just as Tom had.

So in that sense, they were the same. And for the first time in his life he was learning how to give a little, to quit being such a perfectionist and take what he was given with appreciation. "At any rate," he reported candidly to his father, continuing their conversation. "I'm beginning to have real sympathy for the noncustodial parent. I see why people go the extra mile and make all the necessary sacrifices to insure their joint-custody arrangements work." Because it was worth it, to him and the child, to see Ryan any way he could.

"I'm glad you've reconciled yourself to the hand fate has dealt you," his dad said in a scratchy voice. "There've been times lately when you've evidenced more strength and patience than I think I could ever have."

Tom warmed at the praise he heard in his dad's tone, and the knowledge that this crisis hadn't irrevocably damaged their relationship, but instead would probably bring them closer together.

In the background, the doorbell sounded. "Dad, there's someone at the door. I've got to go, but I'll call you back in a few days, just to let you know how things are going."

"You do that, son, and if you need anything at all," his dad said gently, "your mom and I are here for you."

They said goodbye and Tom hung up the phone, feeling better about his relationship with his parents than he had in a long time.

When he opened the front door, he was surprised to see Cynthia standing on the front porch. He hadn't exactly been cordial to her the last time they'd seen one another, yet here she was with apology written all over her face. He wondered what she had to be sorry about. He wondered why she seemed so...distressed.

"May I come in?" Her voice was crisp and clear and businesslike. Too businesslike, suddenly, for his comfort.

Feeling his hope that she was there for more personal reasons abate, he nodded and stepped aside to let her in.

"I have something I want to say to you," she began rather stiffly, following him into the living room, her purse tucked beneath her arm. "And then we're both needed over at Judge Mitchum's office. There are some papers we have to sign."

What kind of papers? Tom wondered, although he had no objection to going over to Judge Mitchum's chambers. He'd lately come to the conclusion that Ryan's interests could be served best if he cooperated fully with the court. Maybe if he'd been more businesslike and cooperative about this whole mess in the first place, people wouldn't have been so quick to believe Sally Ann's lies about him. But they had, and sensing there was no going back, no changing things, Tom took a deep breath and decided to not waste anymore time defending himself when he could be working on building his future.

"All right," he said softly, before she could continue, "but there's something I want to say first." He held up a hand, admonishing her to silence.

She was standing in the sunlight filtering in through the blinds. She looked very beautiful, very vulnerable, and very much in need of a hug. He found that gave him all he needed to go on. Pride was nothing when it came to loving her. And he did love her, he knew. He had for some time. "I was wrong to treat you so badly," he began softly.

Her eyes widened in response, and he continued, "I understand why you said what you did that day in court, that you did it because you love Ryan, because you thought you were protecting his best interests—"

"Tom—" At his words, she looked even more anguished and upset than ever.

"Cynthia, hear me out," he said sternly. "This really is important." He took a deep breath, hoping against hope it wasn't too late, that he hadn't blown everything with his do-or-die attitude toward life. "I was wrong to turn my back on you." His voice had become unaccountably husky. He closed the distance between them and cupped his hands around her arms. "Especially now, when I've never needed or wanted to be with anyone more. I know I blew it where Ryan's concerned," he confessed emotionally, holding her lightly in front of him, though she'd shown no signs of wanting to bolt. "I should've stopped being so selfish, of thinking only of myself, and negotiated a joint-custody arrangement with Sally Ann while the possibility still existed. I should have listened to you and my folks—" he shook his head "—but I didn't. And now it's too late for me and Ryan to be together with the constancy we might have had." His throat closed as he thought of the finality of Judge Mitchum's decision.

Aware he was blinking back tears, and that she looked ready to cry, too, he went on, "But it's not too late for us." Not wanting her to say no, he tucked a hand under her chin and lifted her face to his. The tears she'd been holding back ran freely down her cheeks.

His heart ached at the sight. "I'm trying to tell you that I love you," he whispered hoarsely. Unable to help himself, he touched the softness of her cheek and rubbed it gently with the back of his hand. "And I know now that I always will." And, he thought, that he wouldn't forget her no matter how much he tried. "I know, you've got no reason to want to get involved with me...."

"I've got every reason," she said, moving forward and wrapping her arms around his waist. "Because I love you, too, you fool, more than I could ever say." She gave a little hiccup and smiled through her tears. "I would've been here sooner, to tell you, but I thought you needed time to be by yourself, after everything that's happened."

He lowered his face to hers. "I did," he murmured, both thumbs tracing circles on her face, wiping away the dampness. "But I don't anymore. Now all I need is you."

Later, he didn't remember much about how they got to his bedroom, just that they were there, and that it seemed incredibly right. Emotions too long contained found a vent in the sweetness of their lingering kisses. A thousand feelings flooded him and he welcomed the strength of the woman in his arms, her solidness, her capacity for giving. She was with him once again, and all was right with the world.

This was a new beginning for both of them, and they made love fiercely and passionately. When it was over, they quietly held each other and caught their breaths. It was only later, when she was still wrapped tightly in his arms, that he remembered the appointment with Judge Mitchum. He glanced at his clock on the nightstand and swore softly.

"What time were we supposed to be there?" he asked.

She looked at the clock, too, just as shaken as he was by the impulsiveness of their actions. "We've got time if we hurry." She was already up and reaching for her clothes. "I allowed myself some extra time because I wanted to talk to you."

Forgetting for a moment their need to hurry, he touched her arm and then drew her around to face him. "So you knew even before I told you I loved you we'd be together today?" he guessed softly.

Her eyes holding his, she nodded slowly. "Let's just say I hoped that would be the case," she said, all the love she felt for him reflected in her hazel eyes. "Some things are meant to be. I think we're one of them. And so is Ryan."

"I think so, too."

She returned the kiss lovingly. When they broke apart, her eyes were serious again. "But there's something else I have to tell you, Tom, something important." She explained to him everything she had discovered, ending with, "Sally Ann has agreed to go for counseling. She also has agreed that you should have sole custody for now, although she wants to see Ryan as much as possible.''

For a moment, Tom was so stunned he couldn't move. He could hardly believe what he was hearing was true. And yet he knew from the joy reflected in her eyes that it was.

Too overcome for words, he took her into his arms and held her against him. She embraced him fiercely, with all the love she had to give. It was another moment or two before they moved apart. Her eyes sparkling, with mischief now, she said, ''Shall we go sign those papers and get your son?''

Tom couldn't think of anything that would make him happier. Except . . .

Was he tempting fate?

Or was this, too, meant to be?

He looked down at her, aware what an important moment this was in his life. ''I've always waited for the perfect time,'' he said huskily. He had to fight to keep his voice even. ''The last time my chance almost passed me by. I'm not willing to let it happen again.''

She looked up at him. The encouragement in her eyes, coupled with the depth of her feelings, helped him go on. ''I want you to be my wife,'' he said solemnly, getting down on bended knee. He wanted to do this right. ''Cynthia, will you marry me?''

Surprising him, then, she got down on her knees, too. Her green eyes sparkled with suppressed humor as she pretended to wrestle with the dilemma. ''Marry you? Now? And just hope that things will work out given time?'' she queried merrily, putting her hands on her hips.

He nodded, aware she was teasing him, but hoping her answer was going to be yes just the same, because at that moment he really didn't know what he would ever do without her. She brought sunshine and sanity into his life in a thousand different ways. He had missed her unbearably the past week, and he had an idea she had missed him, too, just as desperately.

But for right now, he thought, amused by her teasing moue, she was playing damn hard to get. Which was okay, he figured humorously, since he could be patient. Maybe more patient than either of them yet knew.

She clasped a splayed palm to her breast. ''You mean despite your bad temper and your perfectionistic demands, despite the fact that you like to have everything your way and yours alone? Hmmm...''

His tension mounting, he slid a hand ever so casually and enticingly up her spine—in much the same fashion as the hero in one of his books might do. ''We probably will disagree. You'll yell at me.'' He guided her closer. ''And I'll yell at you.'' His lips lowered to hers and lingered, and then finally, after much breath-stealing deliberation delivered a heartfelt kiss. He didn't give up until he felt her melting deliciously against him. ''And then we'll make up,'' he said huskily, his lips still hovering over hers, as his hands blazed a path up her hips, to her waist, and over her ribs.

He stopped, poised for her answer, and drew back slightly.

Clasping her hand around the back of his neck, she brought his head down to hers. "Yes," she whispered, kissing him once again. All the happiness she felt was reflected in her eyes. "The answer, my darling, is yes, yes, yes...."

Epilogue

No sooner had the Bronco pulled up in the drive than the front door opened and Rachel and Tom Harrigan came rushing out. "Hi, Grandma! Hi, Grandpa!" four-year-old Ryan called, already unbuckling his seat belt and tumbling out of the car.

"Slow down there," Tom advised his rambunctious son.

"Okay, Daddy!" Obediently, Ryan changed his run to a skip and seconds later was scooped up into Grandpa Harrigan's arms. He gave him a kiss and a hug and then leaned over to give his grandma one, too. "Well, I do believe you've grown again, Ryan Harrigan!" Rachel exclaimed, her hands on her hips.

"Yep," Ryan said, already squirming to be free. "I had to have new pants last week cause Daddy said my old ones were high water. They were getting so far above my ankles it looked like I was getting ready to go wading."

Rachel and Tom Sr. laughed, then greeted their son and daughter-in-law, who'd been slightly slower at getting out of the car and up the walk.

"How was the trip?" Rachel asked Tom, then not waiting for a reply, took an even closer look at Cynthia, who was wearing a loose pastel yellow smock. "Are you feeling okay?"

Tom grinned. His wife was only four months pregnant, just starting to show, and his mom was already clucking over her like an anxious mother hen.

"I'm fine," Cynthia assured her with a grin. She nodded in the direction of laughter and voices. "I take it the others have already arrived?" The annual Easter reunion was a much-loved Harrigan family get-together, one of several held throughout the year.

Rachel nodded. Before she could say more, a little girl in long blond pigtails came dashing around the front. "Hey, Ryan!" Kimberly called excitedly. "You're just in time! We're gonna play tag, and then Grandma says we can have an Easter-egg hunt outside."

Rachel smiled at Tom. "Guess who gets to hide the eggs?"

Tom smiled back. "I don't know, Mom," he said, deadpan, knowing full well the chore was going to be given to him and Mike, as it was every year. Why, he had yet to figure out; he just knew it was expected of him and he enjoyed it. "That one'll require a lot of thought," he added dryly.

"Maybe for you," his younger sister said sassily, rounding the corner of the house. She winked at Cynthia. "Poor Tom here always was a little slow."

"Ha!" Tom said, and the ritual round of good-natured familial insults began as hugs and greetings were exchanged all around.

Together, they moved inside, and from there to the beautifully landscaped backyard where the rest of the clan was gathered. Tom was heartened to see Mike and Diana looking so well. Their first child, Mikey, was in kindergarten now and every bit as lively and precocious as they'd expected. Like Tom and Cynthia, they were expecting a second child of their own. Their three foster sons were all doing well, too. Ernie was finishing up high school and planning a career as an artist. Carlos was in vocational school, learning carpentry. Kevin was currently enrolled at nearby Rice University in Houston, where he was studying computer science and astronomy. Diana had just been reelected for another term as justice of the peace. Mike had expanded the ranch, adding boys and married live-in counselors in equal increments.

His younger sister was doing well, too, Tom was glad to hear. Ross and Linda's preschool was flourishing. Kimberly was doing well in school, and had turned out to be quite a soccer player and pianist in her spare time. He knew Linda was thinking seriously about having a baby, and that Ross and Kimberly were delighted with her decision.

"Everyone looks so happy, don't they?" Cynthia remarked, coming to stand next to Tom.

He nodded, watching Ryan romp with two of his cousins in the grass. Nearby, Mike's three older sons talked sports with Mike and Tom Sr.

Diana and Linda were laughing at the stories Rachel was telling about her two boys, and the scrapes they had gotten into in their youths.

"Yes, they do. What about you?" Tom turned to Cynthia, who seemed to get more beautiful with every passing day. If he'd asked for perfection, which he hadn't lately, he couldn't have gotten a kinder, more loving, more understanding wife. "Are you content?"

Cynthia tilted her head to the side comically. She pretended to give his question some thought. "I don't know," she said. "I always thought I would be content with just two children. But now three's looking awfully good, Tom."

He arched a brow. "Careful, lady," he warned, laughing. "I just might hold you to it."

"You do that, Mr. Harrigan. You just do that." She stood and pressed a kiss to his lips. "Because I don't think I'm going to change my mind." Her hand clasped warmly in his, she moved closer, and like him was content to take in the scene before them for a few more minutes.

Tom thought of all he had been blessed with. "You know," he murmured reflectively, "you were right. Things do have a way of working out, given enough time and patience."

She slanted him a glance. "You're thinking about Sally Ann now, aren't you?" she said softly, seriously.

Tom nodded. It had been a struggle for Sally Ann, but she'd completed her counseling sessions and emerged a stronger, more forthright woman. "She's been good for Ryan, and I know he loves her." The two saw each other whenever possible.

Cynthia smiled warmly. "I like her new husband, too."

Tom nodded in agreement. He, too, liked the down-to-earth widower Sally Ann had married, as well as his four children. "She always wanted a family of her own. Now she has one." And because of that, and the mutually supportive, very relaxed joint-custody agreement they had forged, she was content. Ryan still spent most of his days and nights with Tom because Sally Ann worked outside the home, but she could see Ryan whenever she had time—which was almost every day. And when they couldn't see one another, they spoke on the phone. One way or another, Ryan always knew he was loved by both his parents, and his stepparents. And that was the way they thought it should be.

Tom and Cynthia were silent again, exchanging thoughtful glances. He was aware all over again of how much he loved Cynthia, and she him. It seemed that together, they truly had everything. All his siblings did. And Cynthia's mother was doing well, too. Although she never regained full use of her right hand, Faith was in high demand as a lecturer on flute. Her master classes on flute performance—where she instructed rather than demonstrated—were also in high demand. Cynthia was very proud of her, as was Tom. He knew there were many who never would've risen above the daunting disability, but somehow Faith had. And in his wife he saw the same inner strength.

Beside him, Cynthia stirred slightly, moving closer to his warmth. His glance dropped to her gently rounded silhouette. "What do you think?" he asked softly, placing a hand on her stomach. "Girl or boy?"

"I don't know and I don't care," Cynthia said softly. She placed her delicate palm over his, as if to show that the child growing within her was twice protected, twice loved. "Girl or boy, we'll love the new baby like crazy. And so will Ryan."

"I know," he said, tenderness filling his heart. "And so will the rest of the Harrigans." He nodded to the happy clan scattered over the landscaped lawn.

Cynthia grinned, prophesizing, "We'll all be one big happy family."

Tom nodded agreeably. One big happy family indeed....

HARLEQUIN
American Romance

COMING NEXT MONTH

#337 RETURN TO SUMMER by Emma Merritt

Of all The Stanley Hotel's legends, none was more tragic than that of the whirlwind courtship and brief marriage of a famed Irish singer, Caitlin McDonald, and a dashing race car driver, Blaze Callaghan. History professor Kate Norris played Caitlin at The Stanley's musicale each year, only this time she truly stepped back in time. Did Kate imagine it all? Or did the past beckon to her, promising the key to the love that would always be her destiny?

Don't miss the final book in the ROCKY MOUNTAIN MAGIC series.

#338 SPIKE IS MISSING by Elda Minger

Spike, the million dollar spokescat, had taken a powder. Ad exec Gillian Sommers was given the job of finding the fabulous feline before her biggest client got wind of the disaster. Despite Gillian's objections, Spike's trainer Kevin MacClaine was also assigned to the job. Kevin claimed she was an uptight workaholic who didn't know how to have fun—a catalog of faults Gillian hotly denied.

#339 EVERYTHING by Muriel Jensen

When ex-model Marty Hale bought her family's business, Shannon Carlisle thought he'd be glad of her help in running the department store. But Marty needed help of a different kind. With four boys, a dog and a housekeeper who unfortunately wasn't superhuman, Marty's domestic life was chaos. Shannon didn't want to hurt them, but she didn't know how to be a wife and mother. What on earth was she going to do?

#340 RAINBOW'S END by Kay Wilding

When Quint Richards answered the door of Miss Maudie's stately Georgia home and explained that he lived there, Thea Cameron fainted. Weary and flat broke, Thea and her two sons had traveled for weeks, hoping that Thea's favorite relative would take them in. But Aunt Maudie was convalescing from a broken hip and it was Quint who invited Thea to stay awhile. Thea knew that she would have to leave before he discovered the truth: that he, the local district attorney, shared the house, shared his life—with a criminal.

H A R L E Q U I N
American Romance®

Live the

Rocky Mountain Magic

Become a part of the magical events at The Stanley Hotel in the Colorado Rockies, and be sure to catch its final act in April 1990 with #337 RETURN TO SUMMER by Emma Merritt.

Three women friends touched by magic find love in a very special way, the way of enchantment. Hayley Austin was gifted with a magic apple that gave her three wishes in BEST WISHES (#329). Nicki Chandler was visited by psychic visions in SIGHT UNSEEN (#333). Now travel into the past with Kate Douglas as she meets her soul mate in RETURN TO SUMMER #337.

ROCKY MOUNTAIN MAGIC—All it takes is an open heart.